The Taniwha's Secret

Morgan B. Blake

Published by CopyPeople.com, 2024.

Table of Contents

The Awakening of the Taniwha 1
The Guardian of the Bay 5
The Taniwha's Secret 9
Taniwha's Curse 13
The Taniwha and the Fisherwoman 17
Taniwha's Song 21
The Taniwha's Trial 25
The Taniwha's Pact 29
The Lost Taniwha 33
The Taniwha and the Warrior 37
Taniwha in the River 41
The Taniwha's Revenge 45
The Taniwha's Reflection 49
The Taniwha's Guardian 53
Taniwha and the Brave Fisherman 57
The Taniwha's Mating Dance 61
The Taniwha's Mark 65
The Taniwha's Dream 69
The Taniwha's Betrayal 73
The Hidden Taniwha 77
Taniwha and the Earthquake 81
The Taniwha's Lullaby 85
The Taniwha's Waterfall 89
The Taniwha's Love 93
The Taniwha's Curse 97
Taniwha's Vow 101
The Taniwha and the Ancient Tree 105
Taniwha of the Desert 109
The Taniwha's Gift 113
Taniwha in the Mist 117
The Taniwha's Lantern 121

The Taniwha's Hoard 125
The Taniwha and the Lost Village 129
Taniwha and the Warlord 133
The Taniwha's Reflection 137
The Taniwha's Mirror 141
Taniwha's Return 145
The Taniwha and the Rainmaker 149
Taniwha's Blessing 153
The Taniwha's Embrace 157
Taniwha and the Stargazer 161
The Taniwha's Lair 166
Taniwha's Legacy 170
The Taniwha and the Moonlit Cove 174
Taniwha's Hunt 178
The Taniwha and the Fisherman's Daughter 182
The Taniwha's Homecoming 186
Taniwha's Curse 190
The Taniwha's Challenge 194
The Taniwha's Bridge 198
Get Another Book Free 202

Created by the CopyPeople.com[1]
All rights reserved.
Copyright © 2005 onwards.
By reading this book, you agree to the below Terms and Conditions.
CopyPeople.com[2] retains all rights to these products.
The characters, locations, and events depicted in this book are fictitious. Any resemblance to actual persons, living or dead, events, or locations is purely coincidental. This work is a product of the author's imagination and is intended solely for entertainment purposes.

All rights reserved. No part of this book may be reproduced, stored in a retrieval system, or transmitted in any form or by any means—electronic, mechanical, photocopying, recording, or otherwise—without the prior written permission of the publisher and the author, except in the case of brief quotations embodied in critical articles and reviews.

The views and opinions expressed in this book are those of the characters and do not necessarily reflect the official policy or position of the author, publisher, or any other entity. The author and publisher disclaim any liability for any physical, emotional, or psychological consequences that may result from reading this work.

By purchasing and reading this book, you acknowledge that you have read, understood, and agreed to this disclaimer.

- Thank you for your understanding and support.

Get A Free Book At: https://free.copypeople.com

CopyPeople

---

1. https://copypeople.com/
2. https://copypeople.com/
3. https://free.copypeople.com

The Awakening of the Taniwha

A shimmering moon hung low over the forgotten lake, casting a silvery glow across the glassy surface. Lily, Tom, Jack, and Sara stood at the edge, staring at the dark water. This was their escape, their secret hideaway—a place untouched by time and modern life. They had spent countless weekends here, swimming, picnicking, and whispering about dreams that seemed too big for the ordinary world. But tonight felt different. The air was thick with something unspoken, something ancient, like a pull from the depths of the earth.

"We shouldn't be here tonight," Lily said, her voice hesitant. She pulled her jacket tighter around her, as though trying to ward off a chill that wasn't there. She had heard the old stories—tales told around campfires, whispered warnings about the taniwha that lived in these waters. But they were just stories, right?

Tom laughed, the sound echoing into the night. "Oh come on, Lily, don't be so superstitious. It's just a lake. What's the worst that could happen?"

"I don't know. It just feels... wrong." She crossed her arms, her gaze fixed on the moonlit water.

Jack rolled his eyes. "You're just afraid of a ghost story. It's nothing. Besides, we've come this far. Might as well see what's at the bottom."

Sara, ever the adventurous one, smirked. "Exactly. There's no harm in exploring, right?"

The group gathered their things and started down the overgrown path toward the water's edge. As they reached the old wooden dock, its planks creaked underfoot, worn by years of disuse. No one had been here in ages, but tonight the urge to explore felt too strong to resist. Tom knelt by the dock's edge, peering into the black water.

"Look at this," he muttered, his fingers brushing against something cold and smooth beneath the surface.

Lily took a step back. "What is it?"

"It's a stone. It doesn't look natural." Tom yanked it free, holding it up. It was smooth and carved, ancient-looking, with markings that no one could decipher. "Guys, this is... weird."

Sara's eyes sparkled. "Maybe it's a treasure. Let's keep it."

But as soon as Tom handed the stone to her, the water around the dock began to ripple, as though a giant had just stirred beneath the surface. The moon, which had been so bright moments ago, seemed to dim, as if the very air had thickened. For a long moment, no one spoke. Then, slowly, the ripples spread, growing wider, more chaotic, until the lake began to churn.

"Something's wrong," Lily whispered, her voice trembling.

Suddenly, a low rumble vibrated through the ground beneath them, and the water at the center of the lake began to bubble furiously. The surface cracked open, and with a roar that shook the air itself, a massive figure shot up from the depths.

The taniwha.

Its eyes, glowing with an otherworldly fire, fixed on the group. Its body was covered in scales that shimmered with the light of the moon, and its long, serpentine form twisted and coiled like a serpent that had been awakened from a millennia-long slumber. A deep growl rumbled from its throat as it glared down at them, the very air around them thick with ancient power.

Tom stood frozen, eyes wide with disbelief. "This... this isn't real."

But Sara was already backing away, her eyes wild with panic. "We need to leave. Now!"

The creature's gaze followed her every movement, its massive body swaying in the water. For a moment, it was as though time had stopped, the world around them holding its breath. The taniwha's eyes glowed brighter, and then, without warning, it let out a deafening roar.

The ground beneath their feet trembled as the beast surged forward, its tail sweeping through the water with immense force. Sara screamed and turned to run, but before she could take a single step, the lake seemed to rise up in a great wave, crashing down toward them.

"RUN!" Jack shouted, grabbing Sara's arm and pulling her toward the path.

But the wave wasn't the only danger. As they turned to flee, the trees around them began to sway violently, their branches snapping like brittle bones. It was as though the whole forest had come alive, enraged by the taniwha's awakening. The group sprinted toward the trail, barely keeping ahead of the relentless surge of water and the shrieking wind that followed.

They didn't stop running until they reached the edge of the forest, breathless and disoriented. The sound of the taniwha's roar faded behind them, but the ground beneath their feet still vibrated with its fury. Lily dropped to her knees, hands trembling.

"We need to go back," she panted. "We can't just leave it like this. We... we have to do something."

"No," Tom said, his voice firm. "We need to forget this ever happened. There's nothing we can do to stop it."

But Jack was already shaking his head. "We can't just leave the taniwha there, forever trapped in that lake."

Lily stood up, wiping tears from her eyes. "It's our fault. We woke it up. We have to make things right."

The group stood there for a long moment, the weight of what they had unleashed pressing down on them. Then, without another word, they turned and headed back toward the lake. They knew that they had to face whatever waited for them in the darkness.

When they reached the lake, it was eerily still. The taniwha had disappeared into the depths once more, leaving no sign of its presence. But in the center of the water, where the beast had risen, a strange glow emanated from the depths. The stone, now glowing with an inner light, sat at the water's edge.

"Do you think...?" Sara began, her voice barely a whisper.

"I don't know," Lily said softly, "but maybe the stone has the power to calm it. To put things back the way they were."

Tom reached out and picked it up, his fingers brushing the smooth surface. "It's worth a try."

As he lifted the stone, a sudden rush of warmth filled the air, and the water around them began to settle. The lake, once dark and turbulent, began to calm. Slowly, the ripples faded, and the moonlight returned, casting its soft glow across the water.

But as the taniwha sank back into the depths, a subtle realization washed over them all. The taniwha had not been awakened by the stone. It had been awakened by their own fear—their desire to conquer the unknown, to control what they could not understand. They had disturbed the balance of nature itself. And now, they could only hope that their actions hadn't irreparably altered the world they had once known.

The lesson was clear. Sometimes, the things we seek to control are not meant to be controlled, and in trying to do so, we risk everything we hold dear. As they turned to leave, the glow of the stone faded, and they knew that the taniwha would rest again—until the next time someone dared to awaken it.

The Guardian of the Bay

In a small coastal village nestled between jagged cliffs and the ever-churning ocean, the Taniwha was more than just a legend. It was the protector of the bay, a mighty creature whose very presence kept the storms at bay and ensured the safety of the villagers. The villagers had long revered the Taniwha, knowing that their lives were entwined with the creature's wellbeing. Every year, as the harsh storms of winter approached, they would offer their gratitude with gifts of food, trinkets, and songs, hoping to keep the protector strong for another season.

This year, however, something was wrong.

It started with a strange stillness in the bay. For weeks, the waves had been oddly calm, not the usual wild crashes against the rocks. Then, the signs became more obvious: the Taniwha, which had always been a silhouette against the horizon, no longer appeared. The villagers began to worry. Without the Taniwha to guard them, the storms would come. The village would be lost.

Elder Moana, the wisest among them, called a meeting of the village council. "The Taniwha is ill," she said with a grave expression, "and without it, we are vulnerable. If we don't act quickly, we will face the fury of the sea like never before."

Tane, the village healer, stood up, his face drawn with concern. "What can we do? The Taniwha is no ordinary creature—it is bound to the very soul of the bay. If it is sick, we cannot simply treat it like any other ailment."

"I know," Moana sighed. "But I believe there is a way. There is an ancient remedy, a rare herb known as the 'Moon Blossom' that can heal even the deepest of wounds. It grows in the heart of the Forbidden Forest, beyond the cliffs to the north. But no one has dared venture there in many years. The forest is cursed, they say, filled with dark magic and traps for the unwary."

Tane's eyes narrowed. "I will go. If there is even a chance, I must try."

The council hesitated but knew they had no choice. Tane, with his knowledge of herbs and potions, was the only one who stood a chance of finding the Moon Blossom. The villagers gathered to see him off, and he set out with little more than his satchel, a knife, and the hope that he could save his village.

The journey was treacherous. As he made his way through the cliffs, the wind began to pick up, and the clouds grew heavy. The storm seemed to follow him, a constant reminder of the Taniwha's absence. He pushed on, determined, until he reached the edge of the Forbidden Forest. It was a place shrouded in shadows, its trees twisted and gnarled, as though the forest itself resented intrusion.

Tane stepped carefully into the darkness, the air thick with an unsettling stillness. The further he ventured, the more he felt watched, as though unseen eyes were tracking his every move. Strange sounds echoed in the distance—whispers that seemed to come from nowhere. He shook off his unease, focusing only on the task at hand.

After what felt like an eternity, he found it—the Moon Blossom. It was nestled among a ring of ancient stones, its pale petals glowing softly in the dim light. But as Tane knelt to gather the precious flower, a low growl vibrated through the air.

He froze, his hand hovering over the blossom. From the shadows, a pair of glowing eyes emerged, and the form of a massive beast stepped into the clearing. Its scales shimmered in the moonlight, its long tail sweeping behind it. The creature was an ancient guardian, its very presence a barrier to those who dared seek the Moon Blossom.

"I have no choice," Tane said aloud, more to himself than to the creature. "The Taniwha is dying. I must save it."

The guardian's eyes seemed to soften, but its stance remained firm. It growled again, this time in a warning. Tane stood up slowly, holding his hands out in a gesture of peace. "I do not wish to fight. I only seek the flower that can heal the Taniwha."

The guardian seemed to consider this, its eyes narrowing. "The Taniwha is more than a protector," it rumbled, its voice deep and ancient. "It is bound to the heart of this land. To heal it, you must understand the source of its pain."

Tane felt a pang of confusion. "What do you mean? The Taniwha is sick. I need the flower to cure it."

The guardian stepped closer, its massive form looming over him. "The Taniwha's illness is not a sickness of the body. It is a sickness of the spirit. For too long, it has been tasked with holding back the storms, but it has forgotten its true purpose. It has become a servant to the villagers, and in doing so, it has forgotten the very nature of its being."

Tane's heart sank. "But the villagers... they rely on it. They need its protection."

"The Taniwha needs to protect itself," the guardian said, its voice low. "You must not heal it in the way you think. The Moon Blossom will not cure what ails it. Instead, you must show the Taniwha that it does not owe its existence to the villagers. It must remember its power, its freedom, its true nature."

Tane stood there, the weight of the guardian's words sinking in. He had come to save the Taniwha, but now he understood that true healing would not come from a flower. The Taniwha needed to reclaim its autonomy, to remember that it was not bound by the expectations of others.

With newfound clarity, Tane thanked the guardian and carefully left the Moon Blossom where it was. He turned back toward the village, not with the herb, but with a new understanding. As he returned to the bay, the winds began to howl, the storm beginning to churn on the horizon. But instead of rushing to appease the creature, Tane gathered the villagers together.

"The Taniwha will not be saved by offerings or gifts," he said, his voice firm. "It is not a servant to us, but a creature of great power. We must learn to respect that. We must allow the Taniwha to return to its true purpose. Only then will it protect us once more."

The villagers, at first confused and reluctant, listened to Tane's words. Slowly, they began to understand. They ceased their constant offerings and prayers, instead finding ways to live in harmony with the sea, respecting its forces rather than trying to control them.

The next day, as the storm reached its peak, the Taniwha emerged from the depths, stronger than ever, its great form casting a shadow over the bay. The storm, though fierce, was no match for the creature's power. It calmed the waters with a single sweep of its tail, and the village was safe.

From that day forward, the villagers no longer treated the Taniwha as a mere protector, but as a sovereign being. And in return, the Taniwha watched over them, not out of obligation, but out of a mutual respect for the balance between them. It was a lesson learned in the heart of the storm: true strength comes not from control, but from understanding and respect.

The Taniwha's Secret

In the small seaside village of Tōpuni, nestled between rugged cliffs and a vast expanse of wild ocean, young Maia spent her days exploring the rocky shorelines. The salty wind and crashing waves were her constant companions, and the call of the sea was a pull she couldn't resist. Her mother often warned her to stay away from the deeper waters, where the currents could be treacherous and the legends of strange creatures lingered. But Maia had always been drawn to the mysteries of the sea, and lately, there had been something unusual about the water near the cove—a shimmering glow beneath the surface, a whisper in the breeze.

One evening, as the sun dipped below the horizon, Maia wandered closer to the edge of the cliffs. The last light of day bathed the sea in golden hues, and as the tide rolled in, something caught her eye—a figure, small and graceful, swimming just beneath the surface of the water. At first, she thought it was a dolphin, but something about it seemed different. The creature was elongated, with scales that glimmered like jewels, and eyes that gleamed with an intelligence far beyond anything she had seen in the creatures of the sea.

Intrigued, Maia waited, watching the figure move gracefully through the water. It didn't seem afraid of her presence, as most sea creatures did. The creature—whatever it was—came closer to the shore, its sleek form cutting through the water effortlessly. Maia knelt by the rocks, her breath catching in her chest as it surfaced for just a moment. Its eyes met hers, and for a fleeting second, she could almost feel its thoughts in her mind. There was a sense of sadness, of longing, and something else—something ancient and powerful.

She reached out her hand instinctively, her fingers brushing the water's surface. To her surprise, the creature did not retreat but instead swam closer, nudging her hand gently, as if beckoning her to come closer. Maia felt an inexplicable pull, as though she had been waiting her whole life for this moment.

"Are you... are you a sea creature?" Maia whispered, her voice barely audible over the sound of the waves.

The creature didn't respond with words, but it seemed to understand. It circled her in a dance, its movements graceful and hypnotic. Maia's heart raced as she followed its movements, enchanted by the creature's beauty and the strange bond that seemed to form between them.

For weeks, Maia returned to the cove, always finding the creature waiting for her, its shimmering form cutting through the water with ease. She never told anyone about her new friend, keeping their secret safe between the two of them. The creature, which she had come to call Tahi, communicated with her through gestures and quiet exchanges, as though it could understand her unspoken thoughts. They shared moments of stillness, as if the world around them had fallen away, leaving only the deep connection between them.

But as time passed, Maia began to notice that there was something off about Tahi. The creature's glow seemed to dim, and there were times when it looked tired, even pained, as if it were carrying a heavy burden. One evening, as she sat on the rocky shore, watching the last rays of the sun fade into the ocean, she saw Tahi struggle to stay afloat. The creature seemed weaker, its movements slower, and its once-bright scales now appeared dull, as though the life force that powered it had begun to wane.

"Tahi, what's happening?" Maia asked, her voice filled with concern. "You're not well."

The creature lingered near the edge of the shore, its eyes reflecting a sadness she had never seen before. It nudged her gently, almost as though it was trying to communicate something—something important.

"I don't understand," Maia said softly, her brow furrowing. "What do you need?"

As if in response, Tahi submerged into the water, its form disappearing beneath the waves. Maia waited, anxiety creeping into her chest. After a few moments, Tahi resurfaced, and in its mouth, it held a gleaming object—an ornate, ancient key made of coral and seashells. The key was unlike anything Maia had ever seen, with intricate carvings that seemed to pulse with a life of their own.

The creature circled her once more, its movements deliberate. It then sank back beneath the water, leaving the key floating gently on the surface.

Maia stared at the key, realization dawning. She knew that the ocean, with all its depths and secrets, had a history long forgotten by the world above the water. The key must unlock something hidden beneath the waves, something Tahi had been guarding for centuries. It had trusted her, had shared this secret with her, and now Maia understood. The creature was not just a guardian of the bay; it was the protector of an ancient treasure—a treasure that must remain hidden from the world.

Without thinking, Maia reached out and took the key. As soon as her fingers closed around it, a strange warmth spread through her body. The ocean seemed to shift, the waves stirring as if they recognized the presence of the key. In that instant, Maia understood the creature's plight. The treasure it guarded had been disturbed, threatened by forces long forgotten. The Taniwha, in its disguise as Tahi, had been tasked with protecting the treasure for generations, keeping it safe from those who sought its power.

As the key pulsed in her hand, the creature emerged once more, its eyes meeting hers with a depth of gratitude. It seemed to be asking her to make a choice—to protect the secret or to let the world know of the ancient treasure buried beneath the waves.

"I don't know what to do," Maia whispered, the weight of the decision heavy on her heart. "If I tell others, it could change everything. But if I don't... you'll never be free, will you?"

Tahi circled her once more, then disappeared beneath the surface, its form slowly fading into the depths. Maia stood there for a long while, the weight of the key in her hand pressing her to make a choice.

In the end, Maia kept the secret. She returned to the village and never spoke of the creature or the key. The sea, though, remained as it always had—wild, mysterious, and full of secrets. Tahi, too, remained, watching over the treasure, its guardian ever faithful. Maia often visited the cove, now more aware than ever of the deep, unspoken bond she shared with the creature, and the lesson it had taught her—that sometimes, the greatest treasures are the ones we keep hidden, not out of fear, but out of respect for the delicate balance between the world and the forces that protect it.

And so, the waves continued to crash, the tides rose and fell, and the Taniwha remained, its secret safe in the heart of the deep blue sea.

Taniwha's Curse

The village of Haroa lay at the edge of a rugged coastline, where the jagged cliffs met the relentless crashing of the ocean waves. For generations, the villagers had lived in harmony with the sea, their livelihoods built on fishing, their homes nestled by the shore. Yet, there was one rule that even the most seasoned fishermen knew to respect—the sacred waters of the Taniwha.

The Taniwha was a great creature, ancient and wise, said to reside in the deepest parts of the bay, guarding a treasure hidden in the ocean's depths. It was the protector of the village, keeping the storms at bay and ensuring the fishing grounds remained abundant. The villagers revered the Taniwha, offering small gifts and keeping a respectful distance from the waters it called home. It was said that to trespass on its domain was to invite misfortune.

But for Kaio, the village's best fisherman, the warnings had long since become superstition. He was a man of the sea, his life defined by the rhythm of the waves and the pull of the tides. He had no time for stories or old wives' tales. He knew the waters, and the idea of an ancient sea creature lurking beneath the surface seemed ridiculous. The fish were plentiful, and the catch was always bountiful. What could a mythical creature possibly do to him?

One afternoon, after a particularly fruitful day of fishing, Kaio noticed a glimmer beneath the surface of the water. It was unlike any fish he had ever seen—larger, shinier, and more elusive. His curiosity piqued, Kaio followed the shimmer into the bay, unaware that he was sailing ever closer to the sacred waters. His heart raced with excitement as he spotted the creature again, this time clearly visible just below the surface, its scales glistening like liquid silver.

Without thinking, Kaio threw his net, determined to capture this unusual fish. It was larger than anything he had ever caught, and the thought of it brought visions of wealth and prestige. The Taniwha's waters were sacred, but Kaio was too enthralled by the idea of the creature's worth to remember the old warnings. He was a fisherman. This was his craft, his livelihood. He would take what he wanted.

As soon as the net hit the water, the air seemed to grow thick with tension. The wind shifted, and a low, rumbling sound came from the depths below. Kaio felt a strange unease creeping into his chest, but his greed overpowered it. He pulled on the net with all his might, fighting against the unseen force that tugged back. For a moment, he thought the water itself was alive, fighting him. But then, with a final pull, the net broke free, and Kaio hauled the shimmering creature aboard his boat.

As he stared at the creature, its scales reflecting the light in an almost hypnotic way, a sudden chill washed over him. The world around him grew quiet, as though the sea itself was holding its breath. And then, from the depths, a voice like thunder rumbled through the air.

"You have taken what is not yours."

Kaio froze, his heart pounding in his chest. The voice seemed to come from everywhere, as if the sea itself was speaking. His eyes darted around, but there was no sign of the creature that had spoken. Then, with a sudden rush, the water around his boat began to churn violently.

A massive shape rose from the depths, dark and immense. It was the Taniwha—its eyes glowing with an otherworldly fire. The creature's scales shimmered like stars, its serpentine body coiling around the boat, its great tail splashing the water with a force that nearly capsized the vessel.

"You dare to steal from me, mortal?" the Taniwha's voice boomed, filling Kaio's very soul with a deep sense of dread. "You have broken the sacred bond between us."

Kaio's mouth went dry. He tried to speak, but no words came. The creature's gaze fixed on him, and in that moment, he understood the ancient power that it wielded.

"I have protected this bay for centuries," the Taniwha continued. "The waters are mine, and those who take from them without respect are doomed to join them. You have violated my trust, and now you will become part of what you sought to take."

With a terrible roar, the Taniwha lunged forward, its massive body crashing against Kaio's boat. The force of the impact sent him sprawling into the water. The cold waves swallowed him whole, dragging him beneath the surface. He struggled to breathe, his arms flailing as the water pulled him deeper into the darkness.

Suddenly, his body began to change. His skin tingled, as though it were being reshaped, his bones aching as they morphed into something unrecognizable. His fingers merged into webbed fins, his legs fused together into a long, smooth tail. His eyes shifted, becoming large and black, able to see in the depths of the ocean. And as his breath slowed, he realized he could no longer breathe the air above.

The Taniwha's voice echoed in his mind, a whisper in the depths. "You will serve the sea as I do. Forever bound to the waters you sought to steal from."

Kaio's body was no longer his own. He was part of the ocean now—his form a fusion of man and sea creature, his soul entwined with the currents. He could feel the ocean's pulse beneath him, the slow, endless ebb and flow of the tides. The weight of the world above him became distant, and he found that he could no longer remember his life on land, his name, or the village he once called home. All that remained was the eternal ocean, vast and unforgiving.

And then, as if from a great distance, he understood the Taniwha's lesson. It was not just the theft of a creature or a treasure, but the theft of balance itself. The sea had its rhythms, its rules, and in breaking those rules, Kaio had disturbed the delicate harmony that had kept the village safe for generations.

Years passed, and the village of Haroa flourished, oblivious to the fate of the once-proud fisherman. The Taniwha still watched over the bay, its power unchallenged, and Kaio, now part of the ocean, became a warning whispered to the younger fishermen. It was said that sometimes, on quiet nights, when the moon was full and the waters glowed strangely, the figure of a man with fish-like eyes could be seen swimming beneath the surface, forever guarding the treasures of the deep.

And the lesson lingered: that greed, no matter how small, would always be met with a price. The ocean had a way of keeping its balance, even if it meant taking back what had once been its own.

The Taniwha and the Fisherwoman

In the small coastal village of Rakahanga, nestled between steep cliffs and the restless sea, there lived a fisherwoman named Hana. She was a solitary woman, her days spent casting her nets into the ocean and her nights alone in her small cottage, the sea's constant roar a lullaby in the distance. The villagers knew her well, but few spoke to her. Hana was independent, preferring the company of the sea to the chatter of others. There was something about the ocean that called to her, something deeper than the need to survive.

One evening, after a long day of fishing, Hana noticed a shimmering glow just beneath the surface of the water. The moon hung low, casting its pale light over the waves, and the sea seemed alive with a strange energy. She had heard the stories, of course—the tales of the Taniwha, a great sea creature said to protect the fishing grounds and the village. But Hana had never seen the Taniwha, nor had she truly believed in it. Still, the strange glow intrigued her.

As she rowed closer to the spot where the light flickered, she felt a chill run down her spine. She stopped the boat and gazed into the depths. That was when she saw it—the Taniwha, its long, serpentine body coiling through the water, its scales glimmering like precious stones. The creature's eyes, deep and ancient, locked with hers, and in that moment, Hana felt a sense of connection she had never experienced before. It wasn't fear she felt, but a deep, unspoken understanding, as though the Taniwha had been watching over her for years.

The Taniwha didn't speak, but it circled her boat slowly, its great form undulating through the water with grace. Hana's heart raced, but she remained still, mesmerized by the creature's beauty. She had heard the elders speak of the Taniwha's guardianship over the bay, but now, as she stared into its eyes, she understood what they had meant. The

Taniwha was not just a protector of the sea—it was a guardian of balance, ensuring that the ocean and those who lived by it remained in harmony.

Over the following weeks, Hana visited the bay every evening, and each time, the Taniwha appeared. It was as though a bond had formed between them, a silent agreement. Hana would fish, and the Taniwha would ensure her nets were full. In return, she offered the creature gifts—small tokens of respect, shells, woven trinkets, or songs sung under the moon. The village, unaware of this growing connection, marveled at how Hana's catches seemed to grow larger, more plentiful, and how the storms stayed away from the bay. Hana, in her solitude, felt less lonely, as though the Taniwha were her companion, her protector.

But as the seasons changed, something shifted within Hana. The village had begun to talk, whispering of her growing fortune, of her abundance. Others, fishermen and traders, began to eye her catches with envy. They wanted the same prosperity, the same easy bounty. The temptation to have more grew inside Hana, and she began to push the boundaries of her relationship with the Taniwha. She began to take more than she needed, casting her nets deeper into the bay, reaping more than the sea could offer. She took from the ocean as if it were an endless supply, no longer considering the balance she had once respected.

One night, after a particularly successful catch, Hana returned to her boat, her hands shaking with greed. The Taniwha appeared, its great form rising from the water with a strange intensity. Its eyes, once gentle, now seemed to hold a deep sadness. The creature circled her boat, but it no longer moved with grace. There was a heaviness in the water, a warning.

The Taniwha did not speak, but Hana could feel its disappointment, its sorrow. She had taken too much, and in doing so, had upset the delicate balance between them. She had taken more than the sea could give, and the ocean itself seemed to be responding, the waves now restless, crashing harder against the shore. The Taniwha's presence had grown darker, its power diminished by the greed that had tainted their bond.

"I'm sorry," Hana whispered, but the words felt hollow, empty. The Taniwha's gaze never wavered, and the sea around them began to stir violently. Hana's heart pounded as she realized the truth—she had pushed too far. She had treated the Taniwha not as a companion, but as a tool, and the balance that had once been so steady was now breaking apart.

As the storm surged, the Taniwha's great tail swiped through the water with a mighty force, knocking Hana's boat from its moorings. She was thrown into the sea, the waves crashing over her, pulling her under. For a moment, she thought she would drown, but then, she felt a familiar presence—the Taniwha had come to her side, lifting her from the depths. The creature's eyes were full of sorrow, but there was something else—an understanding, a resignation. It had done what it could, but it could not undo the damage.

Hana clung to the Taniwha, her body tired and broken by the storm. The sea had taken its toll, and the Taniwha had carried her back to the shore. As they reached the beach, Hana collapsed onto the wet sand, her breath ragged, her body exhausted.

The Taniwha did not stay. Instead, it lingered for a moment, its form rising from the water one last time, its eyes meeting hers with a quiet sorrow. Then, with a flick of its tail, it disappeared into the depths, leaving Hana alone on the shore.

In the days that followed, the storms never ceased. The bay, once calm and welcoming, became turbulent, the waters churning in constant unrest. Hana's fishing grounds, once abundant, became barren. The sea, in its fury, seemed to have withdrawn its gifts. The villagers whispered of the curse, of the wrath of the Taniwha.

And Hana, alone in her cottage, began to understand the true lesson of the Taniwha's gift. The sea was not an endless source to be exploited. It was a force that demanded respect, that needed to be honored, not manipulated. She had taken too much, and in doing so, had broken the trust between them.

Hana never saw the Taniwha again. The sea had become quiet, and her nets remained empty. The villagers, too, noticed the change, and they began to speak of the fisherwoman who had once been blessed by the sea. Some said it was a curse, others said it was just the way of the ocean. But Hana knew the truth: the Taniwha had not been her servant. It had been her teacher. And in the silence that followed, she understood that the greatest treasures are those that are shared, not taken.

Taniwha's Song

Every night, as the moonlight filtered through the trees and the gentle sea breeze swept across the village, Tessa lay in bed, her mind drifting toward a haunting melody. It was a soft, eerie song, a voice not of this world, echoing through the quiet spaces of her dreams. She couldn't explain it—couldn't even remember how it began—but the song was always there, calling to her, deep within her sleep. It was as if the very air sang to her, the rhythm of the waves beneath her, the pulse of something ancient and powerful.

Tessa had grown up near the sea, in the small village of Te Roto, where stories of the Taniwha were as common as the sea breeze itself. The elders spoke of the Taniwha as an ancient sea creature, a guardian of the waters and the lands beyond, a creature whose song could be heard only by those who were meant to find it. But Tessa had never given much thought to the stories. Until the dreams began.

Each night, the melody pulled her deeper into a world of vivid images. She would see the ocean, dark and vast, stretching endlessly into the horizon. She saw flashes of a hidden island, shrouded in mist, its shores covered in soft sands. The song seemed to come from that island, a call that beckoned her in ways she couldn't resist. When she awoke, the song lingered in her mind like a half-remembered tune, beautiful and unsettling, a memory she couldn't quite grasp.

One morning, after a particularly vivid dream, Tessa couldn't ignore the pull any longer. She decided to visit the cliffs that overlooked the bay, to see the waters for herself, hoping to find something, anything, that might explain the strange yearning in her heart. The village was still quiet, the fishermen preparing their boats for the day's catch. Tessa walked along the shore, her eyes scanning the horizon, drawn inexplicably toward the open sea.

As the day wore on, the call of the Taniwha's song echoed in her mind, and she felt the urge to walk further along the coast, toward the farthest point, where the cliffs dropped sharply into the sea. There, where the wind howled and the waves crashed against the jagged rocks, Tessa noticed something unusual—a faint glow in the water, almost as if the sea itself were alive, breathing in rhythm with the song.

Without thinking, she descended the rocky cliffs, her feet sure on the familiar paths, until she reached the shore. The air was thick with salt and mist, and the song grew louder, clearer. It was as if the sea had become a living being, singing to her, guiding her. Her heart raced as she stepped into the water, the cool waves lapping against her ankles. The mist swirled, and she felt a strange sensation wash over her, like a door opening deep inside her soul.

As if by some unseen force, the tide shifted, revealing a small island just off the shore. It was unlike anything she had ever seen before—covered in lush greenery, its shores untouched by human hands. The song, so sweet and haunting, seemed to come from the heart of the island, urging her forward. Tessa, entranced, waded deeper into the water, feeling the sea's cool embrace as it guided her toward the hidden land.

The path through the water was treacherous, but the sea seemed to carry her, moving her gently toward the island. As she stepped onto the soft sands, the song reached its crescendo, and Tessa found herself in the center of an ancient stone circle. The stones were covered in moss, their surfaces etched with symbols she couldn't understand. The air felt thick with magic, and Tessa's breath quickened as she looked around, realizing that she had stumbled upon something far older than anything she could have imagined.

The song came to an abrupt stop.

For a moment, there was silence, deep and all-encompassing. And then, from the shadows between the stones, a figure emerged.

It was the Taniwha, or at least something that resembled it—an ethereal being, not entirely of this world. Its body shimmered like water, its eyes glowing with a pale, inner light. It had the form of a serpent, its long, twisting body coiling gracefully around the stones. Its scales sparkled with the hues of the sea, and as it moved, the very air seemed to shimmer with energy.

"You've found me," the Taniwha said, its voice not in words, but in the same song that had guided Tessa here. The melody was now in her mind, an understanding that filled the space between them.

Tessa stood frozen, her heart racing. "I... I didn't mean to intrude. I've been hearing your song in my dreams. I had to find you."

The Taniwha's eyes softened, and it moved closer, its form undulating through the air with grace. "You were meant to find me. You, who are bound to the sea, who feel the pull of the ancient song. But you must understand... there is a price for seeking what is hidden."

Tessa felt a tremor of unease. "A price?"

The Taniwha nodded, its eyes filled with ancient wisdom. "This island, these waters, they are sacred. They are not for those who seek them out in greed or for their own gain. You've heard the song, yes, but you must ask yourself—why did you come here? Was it to understand, or was it to take?"

Tessa's breath caught in her throat. She had not considered the question. She had come out of curiosity, out of the strange connection she felt with the Taniwha, but was there something deeper? Was it truly for knowledge, or had there been a desire for something more?

The Taniwha continued, its voice soft but firm. "The song is a gift, but it is not meant to be captured. It is meant to guide, not to possess."

Tessa stood in silence, feeling the weight of the Taniwha's words sink deep into her soul. The sea had always been a part of her, but perhaps she had sought to understand it in ways that were never meant for her to grasp. She had come here seeking a connection, but had she been willing to pay the price for it?

The Taniwha's form began to fade, its shimmering body dissolving into the mist. "Go back, child of the sea. Let the song be what it is. Do not seek to control it. It is a force of nature, beyond your understanding."

As the Taniwha disappeared, Tessa stood alone in the circle, the song lingering in her heart. She felt a deep peace wash over her, a new understanding blossoming within her. The sea had its own rhythm, its own mysteries, and sometimes the greatest connection was simply in letting it be.

With a final glance at the empty island, Tessa turned and waded back into the water. The song, though silent now, echoed in her heart, a reminder that some things are not meant to be understood, but simply appreciated for their beauty and their mystery.

The Taniwha's Trial

The village of Henga stood on the edge of a great forest, where the river met the sea in a jagged, shimmering expanse of water. It was a place rich in stories and legends, passed down through generations, whispered in the quiet evenings as the firelight flickered and the smoke from cooking fires swirled into the night. But there was one story that the elders told most often, and one that every villager held close to their heart—the story of the Taniwha.

Old Matua Rangi, the village's eldest elder, was the keeper of the Taniwha's tale. She had lived longer than most could remember, her mind as sharp as the jagged cliffs that framed the village. Her voice, though aged, carried with it the weight of history, and when she spoke, the villagers listened intently. They gathered around her in the longhouse one evening, the air thick with anticipation, for tonight was the night she would tell the story again. But this time, it would be different.

"The Taniwha was once our protector," Matua Rangi began, her gaze faraway, as if she could see the past as clearly as the present. "In the days of our ancestors, when the sea was wild and the land untamed, there was a great creature who ruled the waters. It was the Taniwha, a being of immense power, who watched over the river and the shores. When our ancestors first arrived here, they were lost, hungry, and alone. They did not know how to live on this land, how to survive the storms that would rage and the creatures of the deep that would stir."

The fire crackled in the silence, and Matua Rangi's voice lowered, as if the weight of the story hung heavy in the room.

"But the Taniwha, seeing their plight, offered its help. It taught our people how to fish, how to navigate the seas, how to read the winds. The creature protected them from the storms, and the village thrived. The Taniwha became a part of our blood, our spirit. We, the descendants, have carried its blessing ever since."

The villagers sat quietly, hanging on her every word. They knew the story well, but there was something in Matua Rangi's tone that made this night feel different.

"Now," she continued, her eyes narrowing, "the Taniwha's help is needed again. A great storm approaches—one unlike any we've seen before. The winds have shifted, the sky darkens, and the sea is restless. Our village is threatened once more. But the Taniwha will not offer its protection easily. You must prove yourselves worthy, as your ancestors did."

The room fell silent. The weight of her words hung heavy on the villagers. The storm Matua Rangi spoke of had been whispered about in the winds and the clouds, but hearing it from her lips made it all too real.

"How can we prove ourselves?" asked Tei, a young fisherman, eager and earnest, his eyes wide with the challenge that lay before them.

"The Taniwha demands a trial," Matua Rangi said, her voice grave. "A test of spirit and strength. To receive its help, you must show that you understand the balance between the land, the sea, and the people. Only then will the creature rise to aid you. Only then will the storm be turned back."

A murmur swept through the villagers. There was no question about it—the Taniwha was more than a creature of myth. It was a force of nature, a living spirit that could shape the world itself. But to earn its favor, they would need to prove they had learned the same lessons their ancestors had.

"Who will take the trial?" Matua Rangi asked, her gaze sweeping across the room.

One by one, the villagers stood. Tei, the fisherman, was the first to step forward, his chest puffed with determination. Then came Moira, the healer, her steady hands and calm spirit a grounding presence.

Followed by Hana, the blacksmith, whose strength and fire were unmatched. Each one knew the stakes, and each one felt the weight of their ancestors' expectations.

Matua Rangi smiled, nodding at them. "The trial will take place at the river's mouth, where the sea meets the land. The Taniwha will watch. You will face the storm together."

The next morning, the villagers gathered at the river's mouth. The sky was overcast, the sea churned with increasing restlessness, and the air was thick with tension. The group stood together, united in purpose, as they waited for the trial to begin. The Taniwha, they knew, would reveal itself when it was ready.

Tei stepped forward, his gaze fixed on the roiling waters. "We must stand together. The Taniwha helped our ancestors, and it will help us again. We are worthy."

But as they waited, the storm began to intensify. The winds howled, and the sea grew darker, more violent. The trial had begun.

A shape emerged from the depths of the water, rising like a shadow from the sea, and there it was—the Taniwha. Its massive form stretched across the horizon, its eyes glowing with an ancient fire. It was a sight both awe-inspiring and terrifying, and the villagers knew they were being tested.

Tei stepped forward, his heart pounding. He had to prove himself worthy. But as the Taniwha's gaze fell upon him, he felt something stir within him—a sense of uncertainty. Was he truly worthy? He had always fished for his own gain, always taken from the sea without fully understanding the balance.

Moira, the healer, stepped up next, her hands raised toward the Taniwha. "We are not here for ourselves. We ask not for wealth or power, but for the village, for all who depend on the land and the sea."

The Taniwha's gaze softened, but still, it waited.

Hana, the blacksmith, stepped forward last, her strong arms outstretched. "We are connected to the sea," she said. "We have learned the lessons of the past. We ask for nothing more than the chance to live in harmony."

The Taniwha's eyes glowed brighter, and for a moment, the storm seemed to pause, as if holding its breath. The creature's massive form lowered into the water, and the villagers watched in silence.

Finally, the Taniwha spoke, its voice a deep rumble that reverberated through their bones. "You have shown that you understand. You ask not for power, but for balance. You have learned the true lesson of your ancestors—that the sea and the land are not to be conquered, but respected. You are worthy."

And with that, the storm subsided, the winds died down, and the sea returned to its calm, its waters reflecting the pale light of the setting sun.

The villagers stood in silence, awe-struck. They had passed the Taniwha's trial, not through force, but through understanding. They had learned that true strength lay in balance, in respecting the forces that shaped their world.

As they returned to the village, the skies cleared, and the air grew still. The storm had passed, and with it, the knowledge that the Taniwha's power was not something to be commanded, but something to be earned through wisdom and respect. The village had been saved, not by strength alone, but by the willingness to learn from the past and to honor the balance that connected them all.

The Taniwha's Pact

The village of Kaitoa had always been dependent on the sea. Generations of fishermen had cast their nets into the deep blue waters that surrounded their shores, their livelihoods tethered to the whims of the ocean. For years, the catch had been steady, enough to feed their families and sell in the market, but with each passing season, the sea seemed less generous. Fish grew scarcer, and storms more frequent, leaving the fishermen desperate for a solution.

It was during one of these desperate times that the village elder, Rongo, gathered a group of seasoned fishermen to hear an old, nearly forgotten tale. A tale his grandfather had told him, of a Taniwha that once lived in the waters near their village—a great, serpent-like creature of immense power who had struck a pact with the village's ancestors. In exchange for a bountiful catch, the Taniwha had demanded respect and a certain tribute. The old stories spoke of how the creature's protection had kept the seas calm and the fish plentiful. But there had been a price. The terms of the pact had been lost to time, and no one knew exactly what the Taniwha had demanded in return.

With the village facing lean times, Rongo believed it was time to seek out the creature. The fishermen were skeptical, but desperation had driven them to entertain the idea. They ventured to the bay where the Taniwha was said to dwell, their hearts heavy with doubt but filled with a glimmer of hope. As the sun began to set, casting an orange glow over the water, the fishermen stood on the shore, waiting.

Then, from the depths of the bay, it appeared.

The Taniwha was not like the fishermen had imagined. It was enormous, its serpentine body rising from the water like a living mountain. Its scales shimmered like silver in the fading light, and its eyes—dark and ancient—locked onto them with an intensity that sent shivers down their spines. It spoke, its voice a deep rumble that seemed to come from the very depths of the earth.

"I have been watching you, fishermen," the Taniwha said. "Your struggle is clear, and I am willing to help. But know this: all things come with a price."

Rongo, heart pounding, stepped forward. "We seek your aid, mighty Taniwha. The fish have abandoned us, and the storms have grown fierce. What will you ask in return for your help?"

The Taniwha's eyes glowed brighter, as if considering the offer. "I will grant you a bountiful catch, more fish than you have seen in years. The seas will be full, and the storms will cease. But in return, you must keep your promise to me. Each season, you will bring me a tribute—a token of your respect and your understanding of the power I hold."

The fishermen, desperate for the promise of a better life, agreed without hesitation. They shook hands with the Taniwha, sealing their pact. Over the following weeks, the seas were alive with fish. The fishermen caught more than they could carry, their boats filled to the brim. The village prospered, and the storms seemed to vanish as though the Taniwha had taken them away.

But as the seasons passed, the fishermen began to notice subtle changes. The Taniwha's demands, once simple and clear, grew more complex. At first, it asked for small tokens: a handful of precious shells, a carved stone, a simple chant of gratitude. But then, it asked for more. It wanted the best catch from each season, more than was needed for the village. It demanded rare and difficult-to-find fish that required the fishermen to go further and deeper into dangerous waters. Soon, the Taniwha's requests became burdensome, taking more than the fishermen could spare.

One evening, as the sky darkened with the promise of a storm, Rongo and the other fishermen gathered once again on the shore. They were tired, their boats barely able to carry the weight of the Taniwha's growing demands. The once-bountiful seas had begun to feel like a curse, and the fishermen were beginning to question their pact.

"We've given it everything," one of the younger fishermen, Toma, said, his face drawn with exhaustion. "The catch, the tribute, the sacrifices. But what is it asking for now? How much more can we give?"

Rongo was silent for a long moment, his eyes fixed on the dark horizon where the Taniwha had first appeared. He had begun to see it too—the pattern that was unfolding. The Taniwha had come to them in their time of need, but its demands had grown unchecked. What had started as a simple pact had become a binding contract with no end in sight. The Taniwha was not just taking fish—it was taking their livelihoods, their lives.

"We made a mistake," Rongo murmured, his voice heavy with realization. "The Taniwha's help was never meant to be endless. We became greedy. We wanted more than we needed."

As if in answer to his words, the Taniwha's massive form appeared again, rising from the water, its eyes gleaming in the darkness. "You come to me now, fishermen," it said, its voice cold and echoing. "I have given you everything. And yet, you ask for more."

Rongo stepped forward, his voice steady despite the fear that gripped his chest. "We have given too much. We didn't understand the true cost of our pact. What once seemed like a blessing has become a burden. We ask that you release us from the terms of this agreement."

The Taniwha's eyes flickered with something akin to amusement. "You wish to break our pact?" it asked, its voice deepening. "Do you not understand? Once a pact is made, it cannot be undone so easily. You have taken what you wanted. Now, you must take responsibility for what you have given away."

A sudden gust of wind whipped across the shore, and the waves began to churn violently. The fishermen felt a shift in the air, a sense of inevitability settling over them. They had come seeking help, but in their greed, they had lost sight of the balance that should have guided their actions.

"What is the cost, then?" Rongo asked, his voice firm.

The Taniwha paused, its massive body coiling in the water. "The cost is understanding. It is not just the fish you take, but the balance you disrupt. To undo the harm, you must remember the lesson: that no gift is without sacrifice. You have asked for more than you needed, and now you must give back in return."

The Taniwha's form began to fade into the water, its presence slipping away like a shadow. The storm calmed, the waters settled, and the fishermen were left standing in silence, the weight of their realization settling over them like a heavy fog.

In the weeks that followed, the village returned to its simpler ways. The seas no longer gave in abundance, but the fishermen learned to live within their means, taking only what they needed and giving thanks for what the ocean provided. The Taniwha's blessing had not been an endless resource but a reminder of the delicate balance between need and greed, a lesson they would never forget.

The Lost Taniwha

For years, the legend of the lost city beneath the waves had haunted the dreams of explorers and treasure hunters alike. The city, known only as Vahari, was said to be a marvel of ancient engineering, its towers and streets crafted from stones that shimmered like the stars themselves. It was whispered that the city held treasures beyond imagining, relics of a civilization far older than any known to man. But no one had ever found it. The sea, it seemed, had swallowed Vahari whole, and the Taniwha, the ancient sea serpent, was said to guard its secret.

The search for the lost city had become an obsession for a small group of explorers, led by the intrepid Dr. Isla Greyson. Isla, a marine archaeologist, had spent years studying the old maps, piecing together fragments of the myth, and interpreting the clues left behind by those who had sought the city before her. Her team, a mix of skilled divers and researchers, had scoured every inch of the ocean floor within the boundaries of the city's last known location. And now, they were on the verge of finding it—at least, that's what they believed.

As their ship, *The Perseus*, sailed deeper into the uncharted waters, Isla could feel the weight of anticipation pressing on her chest. The team had already spent weeks searching, combing through the deep with sonar and underwater drones, mapping out an ancient structure that seemed to pulse with an otherworldly energy. It was unlike anything they had ever encountered, and the closer they got, the more they began to feel as though they were being drawn toward something—something immense and unknowable.

By the time they reached the spot where the structure seemed to be hidden, the sea had turned darker, the sky above heavy with a storm that brewed on the horizon. Isla stared at the readings on her monitor, which flickered with static, showing a vast network of stone structures beneath the waves. But something else, something far larger, pulsed in the deep. Her gut told her they were getting closer to the city—but also to something else, something far older and more dangerous.

"Get the diving gear ready," Isla said, her voice barely above a whisper. "We're going in."

The divers suited up and plunged into the water, their lanterns casting eerie glows through the murky depths. Isla, on the deck of the ship, watched anxiously through the porthole. As the divers descended, their lights weaving in and out of the shadowy ruins below, something stirred in the water. A massive shape, too large to be any ordinary sea creature, loomed in the distance.

Minutes passed, but then one of the divers, Alex, sent an urgent signal to the surface.

"Isla, you need to see this. There's something here... It's not just the city. There's something... alive."

Isla's heart skipped a beat as she stared at the monitor. The sonar readings had just spiked, indicating movement—slow, deliberate, and immense. The divers' lights flickered, and Isla's gut tightened with unease.

"What is it?" she asked, her voice tight with tension.

Alex's voice crackled through the comms. "It's... It's like a giant serpent. Its eyes are glowing, and it's circling us. We don't know what it wants. I don't think it's friendly."

Isla's blood ran cold. The Taniwha. The creature from legend.

"Get back to the surface," she ordered, her voice sharp. "Now."

But it was too late. The water around the divers began to churn violently, and the communication feed went dead. Isla watched in horror as the blip of the divers' location disappeared from the screen. The storm above them broke, and the wind howled as the ship rocked violently on the waves.

Suddenly, from the depths, a massive shape surged toward the surface, crashing through the water with a power that made the ship lurch. The Taniwha. Its serpent-like body rose from the ocean, its scales gleaming like obsidian in the storm's fury. Its eyes, glowing with an eerie light, locked onto the ship.

The crew scrambled in panic as the creature coiled around the submerged ruins, its immense form casting shadows over the ancient city that lay beneath. Isla stood frozen, unable to tear her eyes away from the Taniwha. It was magnificent, its body a tapestry of ancient markings that glimmered like the very stars in the night sky. But there was something else—something almost human in its eyes, a deep intelligence that made Isla's skin crawl.

And then, to her shock, the creature spoke, its voice a deep, resonating growl that reverberated through the very hull of the ship.

"You have come for what is mine," the Taniwha said. "The city you seek is not for you. It is a tomb, and it has been buried for a reason."

Isla's heart raced as she stumbled backward. "We're not here to steal anything," she said, her voice trembling. "We only want to learn—"

The Taniwha cut her off with a low hiss. "You seek knowledge. But knowledge comes at a cost. The city holds the secrets of those who ruled the sea, but they did not survive the price of their own power. You, too, must prove you are worthy of what you seek."

The storm raged above them, the wind howling as the creature continued to circle. "The city's power lies in the heart of the ruins. But it is not for you to claim. You must face the trial if you wish to understand its secrets."

Isla swallowed, her mind racing. The Taniwha was not just a guardian—it was the keeper of the city's soul. And now, they were trapped, caught between the creature and the knowledge they had come to find.

"We're ready," she said, though her voice felt small and insignificant against the roar of the storm.

The Taniwha's eyes gleamed. "Then you must walk the path of the lost. Only those who truly understand the cost of knowledge may claim what is hidden beneath."

The sea erupted around them, the Taniwha's form slipping beneath the waves as it vanished into the darkness, leaving the crew shaken and uncertain. The storm subsided almost as quickly as it had come, and the water grew still.

But Isla knew one thing: The Taniwha had not shown them the way to the city—it had shown them the cost of discovery. The path ahead would be one of sacrifice, and the city's secrets, once uncovered, could never be returned.

As the ship sailed away from the mysterious ruins, Isla felt a deep, gnawing understanding. Knowledge, once gained, would bind them forever to the past. And no matter how much they sought, the price would always come due. The Taniwha's trial had just begun.

The Taniwha and the Warrior

In ancient times, when the world was still young and the seas were wild, there was a great warrior named Akarui, known across the lands for his unmatched skill in battle and his unshakable honor. His people, the coastal tribe of Mataroa, had long lived in harmony with the sea, respecting the sacred waters that provided them with sustenance and protection. But the people also feared what lurked beneath those waters—the ancient Taniwha, a creature of immense power said to guard the ocean's secrets.

The Taniwha, it was said, chose one warrior from each generation to become its guardian. The chosen warrior would pledge to protect the sacred waters and ensure the balance between the land and sea. The bond between the Taniwha and its chosen guardian was one forged in the depths of the ocean, stronger than any sword or shield. It was a bond of trust and respect, an unbreakable pact.

When Akarui was chosen by the Taniwha, the elders rejoiced, for they knew the warrior's strength and character. But the choice did not come without sacrifice. Akarui was to leave behind his family, his people, and his life as a warrior on land. For the next ten years, he would serve the Taniwha, guarding the sacred waters, and in return, the creature would ensure the safety of Mataroa.

Akarui accepted the Taniwha's call without hesitation. His loyalty to his people and his respect for the ancient creature were unwavering. He swore an oath before the village and the sea, vowing to protect the waters with his life. And so, he journeyed to the coast, where the Taniwha waited beneath the waves, its presence felt as a shifting current in the depths.

The Taniwha rose from the sea, its great form emerging from the depths like a living mountain. Its eyes glowed with ancient power, and as it gazed at Akarui, the warrior felt a shiver run through him, but not of fear. The bond was immediate, a deep understanding that transcended words. The Taniwha was no mere beast; it was a being of wisdom and grace, as old as the seas themselves.

For years, Akarui and the Taniwha worked together, a perfect partnership. The waters remained calm, the storms stayed away, and the village flourished. Akarui learned the ways of the sea, understanding the tides and currents like never before, and the Taniwha, in turn, respected his strength and courage. They were inseparable, guardians of the land and the sea, bound by the pact they had forged.

But as time passed, Akarui began to notice something that troubled him. The bond between him and the Taniwha, while strong, began to feel suffocating. His days as a warrior had taught him independence and freedom, and the constant vigilance over the sacred waters weighed heavily on him. He missed his people, the battles he had once fought, the thrill of adventure. Though the Taniwha had given him power and purpose, a seed of doubt began to grow in his heart.

One fateful day, the storm clouds gathered on the horizon, darker than any Akarui had seen before. The winds howled, and the sea churned violently, as if the ocean itself was angry. Akarui stood on the edge of the cliffs, watching the approaching storm, when a figure emerged from the shadows. It was a man from his village, a former friend named Kaito, who had once fought alongside him in battles long past.

"Akarui!" Kaito called out, his voice filled with urgency. "The Taniwha is a prisoner of the sea! The storm is a sign—it is angry, and it will destroy everything we hold dear. We must break the bond with the Taniwha before it consumes us all!"

Akarui's heart skipped a beat. "What are you talking about?" he asked, his voice low with disbelief. "The Taniwha has kept us safe for generations. Why would it turn against us now?"

Kaito's eyes were wild, desperate. "You don't understand. The Taniwha has demanded too much from us. The balance has been disrupted. We have given too much in tribute, and it is no longer content. It will not stop until it has everything."

Akarui's mind raced. He had always trusted the Taniwha, but Kaito's words stirred something within him. Could it be true? Had the Taniwha's demands grown too great? Was the creature no longer the protector it had once been?

"Kaito, you must be mistaken," Akarui said, but doubt gnawed at him. The storm was growing stronger, and the sea raged with fury. "But... what if you're right? What if the Taniwha's power is no longer a blessing?"

In that moment, a decision was made. Akarui, torn between loyalty and doubt, followed Kaito's lead. They made their way to the shore, where the Taniwha waited beneath the roiling waves. The creature rose from the depths, its form dark and ominous, its eyes glowing with an unearthly light.

"You have broken the pact," the Taniwha's voice rumbled, its words carrying a weight that shook Akarui to his core. "You question me? You seek to betray the bond we forged?"

Akarui's heart pounded. "I—no, Taniwha. I only sought to protect my people. I thought... I thought you were turning against us. But now I see..." His words faltered, his voice breaking. "I have failed you."

The Taniwha's eyes softened, and for a brief moment, Akarui saw the creature as it had been: wise, powerful, and protective. But the storm continued to rage, and the bond between them was slipping away.

"Your heart was true, Akarui," the Taniwha said. "But you were blinded by fear. The true cost of our bond was never in the sacrifices made—it was in the trust that we shared. You have broken that trust, and now, the balance has shifted."

Akarui dropped to his knees, his sword slipping from his hand. "I failed you," he whispered, tears welling in his eyes. "I betrayed you for fear of what I did not understand."

The Taniwha's massive tail swept through the water, sending waves crashing against the shore. "You are not the first to fail me, Akarui. But you are the first to realize the cost of betrayal. You have learned the greatest lesson of all—the true price of power is not in what we give, but in what we are willing to keep."

With that, the Taniwha disappeared into the depths, and the storm ceased as suddenly as it had begun. Akarui remained on the shore, his heart heavy with the weight of his choices. The bond had been broken, not by the Taniwha's anger, but by his own doubt. He had feared the very thing that had once given him strength—the trust he had in the creature.

Akarui stood alone by the water, his lesson clear. Power, once granted, could not be taken lightly. Trust, once broken, could never be fully restored. The Taniwha had never asked for loyalty or sacrifice—it had only asked for understanding. And in the end, that was the true test.

Taniwha in the River

In the small village of Aroha, nestled between rolling hills and a winding river, young Hemi lived with his family on the outskirts, near the water's edge. The village had always relied on the river for fishing, drinking, and irrigation. But for Hemi, the river was something more—a source of endless fascination. He often spent hours by the water, skipping stones, watching the fish swim lazily beneath the surface, or simply listening to the quiet murmur of the current.

One evening, after a particularly long day of chores, Hemi wandered farther downstream than usual, following a narrow path that led deep into the forest. The sky was painted in hues of orange and purple, and the cool evening breeze rustled the leaves. The river was unusually calm, almost unnervingly so. As he stepped closer to the water, a soft sound—like a distant whisper—caught his attention. He froze, his eyes scanning the riverbank.

The whispering grew louder, almost like a melody carried by the wind. It was not the sound of the usual rustling reeds or flowing water. No, this was something different. Something ancient.

Hemi knelt by the water, peering into the murky depths, his heart thumping in his chest. And that's when he saw it.

A pair of glowing eyes emerged from the water. At first, he thought it was a fish, or perhaps an illusion caused by the light. But then, the creature rose slowly, its long, serpentine body coiling through the water. It was massive, its scales shimmering in the twilight. Hemi's breath caught in his throat. He had heard the elders talk of such creatures—of Taniwhas—great beings that protected the land and the waters, guardians of nature's balance. But no one had ever seen one, not in his time, anyway.

The Taniwha regarded him with silent curiosity. Its eyes, ancient and knowing, seemed to search him, weighing him. For a long moment, neither moved. Hemi's instincts told him to run, to flee back to the village, but something inside him, something deep, told him to stay. The creature was not here to harm him. The river was its home, and he was simply an intruder on its domain.

"You see me, boy," the Taniwha's voice echoed in his mind, deep and resonant. "I have watched your people for many years, but you are the first to truly see me."

Hemi blinked, surprised by the voice in his head. "I... I didn't mean to disturb you," he stammered. "I just came to the river. My name is Hemi."

The Taniwha's form shifted in the water, its tail creating ripples that spread through the river. "You are not disturbing me. But now you have seen me, you must understand. I am the guardian of this river, the protector of these lands. But the balance is shifting. Your people... they are taking more than they should. They are using the river, the forest, without giving back."

Hemi swallowed hard. His father was a fisherman, and his mother used the river for farming. Everyone in the village relied on it. "I... I don't understand. We've always used the river. It gives us fish, it gives us water. What do you mean 'taking too much'?"

The Taniwha's eyes darkened. "The river gives, yes. But it asks for respect in return. For centuries, I have ensured that the waters remain full, that the fish are plentiful. But greed has grown in your village. You pollute my waters. You take more than you need. The balance is tipping."

Hemi felt a pang of guilt, though he wasn't entirely sure how he could help. His village had always depended on the river, and it wasn't as if they were intentionally harming it. But he could see the Taniwha's concern in its eyes. The creature was not angry, but sad, almost as if it were weary from its endless task of maintaining balance.

"What do you want me to do?" Hemi asked, feeling small before the immense creature. "How can I fix this?"

The Taniwha's gaze softened. "You are young, but your heart is pure. The answer is simple: you must be the bridge between us. You must help your people understand the true cost of their actions. You must teach them that the river's gifts are not limitless. Only then will the balance be restored."

Hemi didn't understand what the Taniwha meant at first, but the creature's words echoed in his mind long after the encounter. Over the next few days, he couldn't shake the feeling of responsibility weighing on him. The river had always been the lifeblood of the village, but he had never truly considered the price it exacted. The thought of the Taniwha's disappointment gnawed at him.

That night, he spoke with his father, who had spent years fishing the same stretch of river.

"Father," Hemi said, "we've taken so much from the river. The Taniwha... the guardian of the river, says we're harming it. We're not respecting it. We have to change."

His father looked at him as if he had lost his senses. "What nonsense is this, Hemi? The river provides us with everything we need. Your grandfather fished these waters, and his grandfather before him. You can't believe in such fairy tales."

But Hemi persisted. He spoke of the Taniwha, of what it had said, of the need to give back, to restore balance. He wasn't sure if his words would carry weight, but he had to try.

Slowly, word spread through the village, and a few others began to listen. Together, they started cleaning the river, removing the pollution that had accumulated over the years. They planted trees along the banks to prevent erosion, and they learned to fish in moderation, taking only what they needed and never more. It wasn't easy. There was resistance, of course—many villagers believed they had always fished and farmed the way they had, and that it was the natural order of things. But in time, the younger generation, including Hemi's friends, rallied around him.

Weeks passed, and slowly, the river began to change. The water cleared, and the fish returned in greater numbers. The Taniwha, Hemi could feel, was pleased. One evening, as the sun dipped low over the water, the creature rose from the depths once more, its eyes gleaming with a quiet pride.

"You have done well, boy," it said, its voice softer now, as if the weight of centuries had lifted. "You have restored the balance, and in doing so, you have saved both your people and the river."

Hemi smiled, but as the Taniwha disappeared beneath the waves, he realized something deeper. The true lesson was not about protecting the river or saving the Taniwha—it was about the responsibility that came with taking what nature offered. The river's gifts were never given freely; they were part of an eternal cycle, one that required respect and understanding. In giving back, in restoring the balance, the village had found harmony with the world around them.

And with that, Hemi understood. The true cost of living, of survival, was always respect—the respect for the land, the water, and the creatures that sustained them. Without it, nothing would thrive.

The Taniwha's Revenge

The sea was calm when the treasure hunters first sighted the island, but the air was thick with the promise of danger. Captain Elias Ashford stood on the deck of *The Wanderer*, his sharp eyes scanning the horizon. Behind him, a crew of men and women bristled with excitement. They had been at sea for months, navigating treacherous waters, following cryptic maps, and deciphering old legends. And now, finally, they had found it—the lost island said to be the resting place of treasures guarded by a great creature, a Taniwha.

"Get the boats ready," Ashford ordered. His voice was low, tinged with anticipation. "Tonight, we claim what's ours."

The Taniwha had been a myth, a tale whispered in port taverns and etched in the pages of ancient scrolls. Some said it was a massive serpent that lived in the deepest parts of the ocean, guarding treasures beyond imagining. Others claimed it was the spirit of the sea itself, a force of nature that could befriend those who respected the waters or destroy those who dared to disturb its peace. Ashford didn't care for legends—he cared for gold. The island had been marked on the map, and if the stories were true, they would find unimaginable riches below its shores.

The crew rowed their boats toward the darkened beach, the waves lapping against the hulls with an eerie stillness. The moon was high, casting long shadows over the jagged rocks and thick jungle that awaited them. Ashford led the way, his heart pounding with excitement as they disembarked. The treasure was said to be hidden beneath the island, guarded by the Taniwha itself. But the crew was unfazed. They had come for treasure, and nothing would stand in their way.

They set to work, digging and clearing the earth, following the coordinates they had painstakingly decoded from an old, tattered journal. As the hours passed, they found nothing but soil and stone. But then, as the first light of dawn broke through the trees, one of the crew members, a young man named Bran, cried out in triumph.

"I found it! The entrance!"

The crew gathered around as Bran cleared away the last of the debris, revealing a stone doorway carved with intricate symbols. There was no mistaking it. This was the tomb of the Taniwha. Ashford's pulse quickened as he stepped forward, pushing the heavy door open with a groan. The air that escaped from the darkened passage was thick with the scent of age, damp and musty, but beneath it all was something else—a lingering power, as if the earth itself was alive.

They descended into the depths of the cave, their lanterns flickering in the darkness. The walls of the tomb were covered in ancient carvings, images of the Taniwha coiling through the sea, wrapped around treasures, and watching over the island. At the heart of the chamber, they found it—a chest, covered in gold filigree and encrusted with gemstones that sparkled in the dim light. Ashford grinned as he stepped forward, his fingers itching to pry open the chest.

But just as he reached for the lock, the ground trembled. A low rumble shook the air, and the water that surrounded the island began to churn. A deep, guttural roar echoed from somewhere below, and the temperature in the cave seemed to drop. The Taniwha was near.

"Grab the treasure!" Ashford shouted, his voice frantic. "We don't have much time!"

But before they could move, the earth shook again, harder this time. The chest rumbled violently, and the cave ceiling above them cracked. Dust and debris fell in torrents, and the roar grew louder, filling their ears with a primal fury. The walls of the cave seemed to pulse, as if the very heartbeat of the island had awakened.

Suddenly, the entrance to the tomb was blocked by falling rocks, trapping them inside. The hunters turned to Ashford, panic rising in their chests.

"What's happening?" Bran shouted, his voice shaking. "The Taniwha—"

"Get the chest!" Ashford ordered, his voice now tight with fear. The storm above, the rumblings beneath their feet—it was clear. The Taniwha was coming for them.

But it was already too late. The rumbling intensified, and the sound of the sea crashing against the rocks echoed from every direction. With a deafening roar, the Taniwha burst forth from the depths, its massive form crashing through the water. The sea surged violently, waves crashing against the shore as the creature's massive body emerged from the depths. Its eyes, glowing with an ancient fire, locked onto the treasure hunters with a fury that could only be described as vengeance.

Ashford and his crew scrambled, trying to escape, but the entrance to the tomb was blocked. The Taniwha's enormous tail swept through the water with the force of a storm, sending shockwaves through the cave. The treasure hunters were tossed aside, their efforts to escape futile. The chest, the treasure they had risked everything for, was forgotten in the face of the creature's wrath.

With a sudden crash, the waters surged upward, filling the cave. The Taniwha, towering above them, roared once more, shaking the very foundations of the island. The cave began to collapse, the ceiling cracking and falling apart. In that moment, Ashford realized the truth—the Taniwha had been guarding something far more valuable than gold. It had been guarding the balance of the island, and those who had come to steal had tipped the scales beyond repair.

The storm outside intensified, and the waves, now violent and unforgiving, swallowed the shore. The ship they had arrived on, *The Wanderer*, was no longer visible. Ashford's heart sank as he watched the water rise, the roar of the Taniwha's fury filling his ears.

As the water reached their knees, then their waists, then their chests, Ashford and his crew knew it was over. The Taniwha's vengeance had been swift and complete. The price of greed had been paid in full.

And as the last of the treasure hunters were swept away by the rising tide, the island fell silent, the Taniwha returning to the depths, its ancient charge fulfilled. The treasure was never claimed, and the river of the island returned to its peaceful flow. The balance had been restored, but the lesson would linger for anyone who came after—greed may promise riches, but it would always exact its price from those who dared disturb the natural order.

The Taniwha's Reflection

For centuries, the Taniwha had been the guardian of the great lake, a creature of immense power whose scales shimmered in the moonlight, and whose presence was felt in every ripple of the water. Its form, serpentine and monstrous, was feared by all who lived nearby. The villagers of Khara spoke of the Taniwha in hushed tones, telling stories of how it could both protect and destroy, its moods as changeable as the winds themselves. But no one truly understood the creature, nor dared approach the sacred waters where it roamed.

Yet one day, the Taniwha was cursed.

The curse came from a sorcerer, a man who had grown envious of the Taniwha's power. He was tired of hearing the villagers speak of the Taniwha's grandeur, tired of seeing its name revered. He wanted that power for himself. The sorcerer, with all his dark magic, cast a spell that trapped the Taniwha in the form of a human. Its great form was gone, replaced by a man—tall, broad-shouldered, and with eyes that still held the reflection of the serpent's vast depths. But the spell twisted its essence, and the man found himself trapped in the human body, unable to return to his former self.

The villagers found him wandering near the outskirts of the lake, lost and confused, his eyes flickering with the faintest trace of the Taniwha's soul. He was a man, but there was something monstrous about him—something unsettling in his gaze. They saw only the reflection of the beast they had feared, and with great fear and suspicion, they rejected him. They called him a demon, a thing born of nightmares, and chased him from their homes.

For many years, the cursed man lived alone, hiding in the woods and by the lake, never able to return to the water that had once been his home. He could no longer feel the comforting ripple of the currents, no longer swim through the deep, murky waters of his old world. Instead, he was bound to the land, a creature of flesh, his heart aching with the loss of his true self.

One evening, as the sun dipped low behind the mountains, casting long shadows over the village, a young woman named Lira made her way to the lake. She had heard stories of the man who had appeared near the water, the one the villagers whispered about. But unlike the others, she was not afraid. Lira had always been different. She had spent her life tending to the sick and the wounded, offering her help to anyone who needed it, regardless of who or what they were. She had never believed the stories the villagers told about the Taniwha being a creature of pure evil. She had always wondered if the beast, too, had a story worth hearing.

When she reached the lake, she saw him.

The man was standing by the water's edge, staring out into the deep, his broad frame silhouetted against the fading light. There was something in his posture, something that spoke of loneliness and longing. His eyes, the same strange shade of green as the lake's deepest waters, flickered with a sadness that made Lira pause. She stepped forward, her heart beating a little faster.

"You are the one they call the Taniwha?" she asked, her voice soft but steady.

He turned slowly, his expression unreadable. His human form was imposing, his features sharp and strong, but there was an undeniable gentleness in the way he regarded her. "I was once the Taniwha," he said, his voice deep, but with a hint of sorrow. "But now I am cursed. I am a man, trapped in this form. I cannot return to the water."

Lira studied him for a long moment, her eyes never leaving his. The villagers had told her he was a demon, but she saw something different in him—a quiet pain, a yearning. She didn't see a monster. "You are not what they say," she said quietly, almost to herself.

He looked at her with surprise, as though no one had ever said such a thing before. "What do you see?" he asked, his voice rough, as though he hadn't spoken to anyone in a long time.

Lira stepped closer, her gaze softening. "I see someone who has been hurt. Someone who has been made to carry a burden that is not his own. I see someone who is lost, yes, but not a monster."

The Taniwha's eyes widened, and for the first time in years, a glimmer of hope flickered in his chest. Could it be? Could she, a human, see past the curse? Could someone understand him, even now?

"I can't change what I've become," he said, his voice heavy with regret. "The sorcerer's magic has trapped me here. I cannot return to my true form. I can never be what I was."

Lira's gaze never wavered. "What if you never needed to return to what you were? What if the true nature of someone isn't in their form, but in who they are inside?"

The Taniwha looked at her, his heart pounding. The weight of his centuries of solitude, of rejection and hatred, suddenly felt lighter. She wasn't afraid of him. She saw him—not as a beast, but as someone in pain, someone worthy of compassion. He realized then that the curse was not just in his outward form, but in his own belief that he was nothing more than a monster. He had carried that belief for so long that he had forgotten who he truly was.

Lira reached out a hand, her fingers gently brushing his. The moment their hands touched, something shifted in him. The world around him seemed to slow, and the lake's deep waters reflected not just his human form, but the creature he had once been—his soul unburdened, free to be both man and Taniwha.

The curse, it seemed, was never truly about the form. It was about the self. It was about how one saw oneself, and the acceptance that only comes from within.

"I see you," Lira said, her voice gentle but firm. "You are not a monster. You are just a soul, a soul that has been misunderstood."

In that moment, the Taniwha's form shifted, not into a beast, but into something new—something more than just man, more than just creature. He was both. He was whole.

The curse was broken, not by the breaking of magic, but by the breaking of perception. He had learned that the true nature of a being is not defined by how others see them, but by how they see themselves. The Taniwha's reflection was no longer monstrous. It was a reflection of something true, something honest.

And as Lira turned to leave, she knew the Taniwha was no longer just a legend. He was a soul reborn, free from the curse of self-doubt, forever at peace with the water and with himself.

The Taniwha's Guardian

In the small village of Te Aro, nestled between towering mountains and the vast, untamed sea, there lived a young girl named Marama. She was the daughter of the village healer, raised among herbs, potions, and ancient stories. Her world was one of simple comforts and quiet routines, but there was always something in the air—the weight of a mystery that her elders spoke of only in whispers. The Taniwha.

The Taniwha was a creature of legend, a mighty guardian said to rule the waters where the river met the ocean, protecting both the land and its people. It was a being of immense power, neither entirely human nor entirely beast, and its loyalty was to the natural world and the balance it required. The elders of Te Aro had long warned the villagers not to disturb the sacred lands of the Taniwha. Those who did had never been seen again. The creature, though rarely seen, was known to protect the river and the ocean with a ferocity that spoke of ages-old wisdom.

But Marama had never truly believed in the Taniwha, not as the villagers did. She thought of it as a story, something to warn children to respect nature. Until one day, when she was thirteen, her world changed forever.

It began with a dream. In it, the great Taniwha, coiled like a serpent of the sea, appeared to her in the depths of the river. Its eyes were enormous, glowing with a strange, ancient light. It spoke without words, the message reaching her heart in a deep, resonating voice.

"You are chosen," it said. "The balance of the land and the sea is in your hands now. You will be my protector in the human world."

Marama awoke with a start, her heart pounding, the dream vivid and unsettling. She shook it off, assuming it was just a dream—a product of her growing curiosity about the old stories. But the next day, the signs began to show. The river, which had always been gentle, surged unexpectedly, its waters rising higher than ever before. The birds in the trees began to act strangely, circling above her house, and the air itself felt charged, as if nature itself was watching her.

That evening, as the sun dipped below the horizon, Marama stood by the river's edge. Her heart ached with the feeling that something was about to change, something she could neither ignore nor understand. It was then that she saw it.

The Taniwha rose from the water, its great form breaking the surface like a wave itself. Its scales shimmered in the twilight, reflecting both the ocean and the stars above. Marama's breath caught in her throat as the creature turned its massive head toward her, its eyes still glowing with that otherworldly light.

"You have seen me now," the Taniwha's voice echoed in her mind, deep and powerful. "The balance is tipping. The humans take more than they give, and the land begins to wither. You will be my guardian in their world, keeping them in check, ensuring the natural world is not forgotten."

Marama fell to her knees, overwhelmed by the presence of the Taniwha. "I—I don't understand. I am just a child. How can I protect the balance of the world?"

The Taniwha's gaze softened. "You have always been connected to the land, Marama. Your heart is pure, and you understand the rhythm of life. It is not power that is needed, but wisdom. You must remind the humans of the balance they have forgotten. Only then can the river, the sea, and the land remain in harmony."

As the creature slowly submerged back into the depths, Marama was left standing at the river's edge, her mind swirling with questions and fear. What did it mean to be the Taniwha's guardian? How was she to ensure the balance? She had no answers, only a deep sense of responsibility pressing on her chest.

Days passed, and Marama began to see the changes all around her. The villagers, as always, went about their daily routines—fishing in the river, gathering resources from the forest, and cutting down trees to build their homes. But the land was becoming restless. The crops failed in certain parts of the village, the fish in the river grew scarcer, and even the winds seemed to be growing harsher. Yet no one seemed to notice. They carried on as they always had.

Then came the first warning. The river, which had always been a constant source of life, flooded one night, sweeping away crops and homes. It was the Taniwha's anger, and it was clear. The land had been disrupted, the balance upended, and now, the earth itself was retaliating.

Marama stood by the river the next morning, watching the devastation. She knew what she had to do. She could no longer remain a passive observer. Her role was to speak out, to protect both the people and the land, even if it meant confronting them with the truth.

She approached the village square and spoke to the elders, her voice steady. "The river and the sea are in distress. The balance is broken. The Taniwha has chosen me to restore it."

The villagers laughed, dismissing her words as the fanciful notions of a child. "The river's flood is just nature's course, Marama," one elder said dismissively. "It's nothing to do with your Taniwha."

But Marama did not back down. She began to show them the signs—the wilting crops, the changing weather patterns, the fish that no longer swam where they once did. Slowly, over weeks, the villagers began to listen. It was then that the Taniwha appeared to them, rising from the river to confirm Marama's words. The creature's form, once feared, now stood as a symbol of the earth's voice—a reminder of the balance that had been ignored.

With the Taniwha's blessing, Marama helped the villagers learn to live in harmony with nature once again. They planted trees to replace the ones they had cut down, learned to fish in moderation, and only took from the land what they needed, leaving enough for the future.

But Marama's role was not just to protect the balance. It was to remind the humans of their connection to the earth, to show them that power over nature was never the answer. The Taniwha, in its great wisdom, had entrusted her with the task not just of guarding, but of teaching.

Years passed, and Marama grew into a wise woman, respected by the villagers and revered by those who still remembered the ancient tales. The balance, once restored, held firm, and the river flowed as it always had, calm and steady. The Taniwha's presence, though no longer as visible, remained a part of her life.

One day, as she stood by the river, now an old woman, Marama looked out at the waters, her heart at peace. The lesson had been learned—not through power or force, but through understanding and respect. The Taniwha had given her a gift—a reminder that the world's true strength lies in its balance, and the most important role we play is not as conquerors, but as guardians.

Taniwha and the Brave Fisherman

For generations, the village of Kaiwharangi had lived in peace, nestled on the shores where the river met the sea. The village relied on the bountiful waters for its sustenance, and the people revered the river, its currents carrying more than fish—they carried the lifeblood of the village itself. But with prosperity came complacency, and for years, the villagers had forgotten the ancient warnings. The Taniwha, a creature of unimaginable power, once a guardian of the waters, was no longer honored. The fishermen took too much from the river, the forest was stripped bare to build new homes, and the once-thriving ecosystem began to wither.

The first sign of the Taniwha's displeasure was the storm. It came suddenly, without warning, a tempest that swept across the shores, knocking boats from their moorings and flooding the village streets. The villagers prayed to their gods for mercy, but the storm only grew fiercer. It was in the midst of this chaos that Tane, the village's most respected fisherman, was approached by the village elder.

"You must confront the Taniwha," the elder said, his voice trembling with fear. "It is angry with us. We have taken too much, and now we must face the consequences. Only you, Tane, can end this."

Tane, though brave and strong, had always heard the tales of the Taniwha, the monstrous guardian of the waters. He had grown up fearing the creature's wrath and had never dared venture near the sacred river beyond the village boundaries. But the elder's words left no room for hesitation. The village was in peril, and it was up to him to save them.

Armed with nothing but his courage and a weathered fishing spear, Tane made his way to the river's mouth, where the storm raged fiercest. The winds howled, and the waters churned like a living beast. As Tane approached the shore, the earth trembled beneath his feet. The Taniwha was close.

Then, from the depths, it rose.

The Taniwha's massive form emerged from the river, its body coiled like a serpent, covered in scales that shimmered in the dim light of the storm. Its eyes glowed with an eerie light, ancient and filled with fury. The creature was enormous—so large that it seemed to eclipse the sky itself.

Tane stood frozen, his heart pounding in his chest. He had heard the stories of the Taniwha's wrath, of entire villages being destroyed by its anger. But in that moment, he could see no evil in its eyes—only a deep sadness and frustration.

"I have come to stop you," Tane said, his voice steady despite the fear in his heart. "You have brought this storm. You have caused this destruction. But I will not let you harm my people."

The Taniwha's massive head tilted slightly, as if considering him. Then, in a voice that sounded like the rumbling of thunder, it spoke.

"You misunderstand, brave fisherman," the Taniwha said. "I do not wish to harm your people. I seek only balance. For years, you have taken from these waters, never giving back. The river has become poisoned with your greed. The storm is my warning. If you do not stop, it will be the end of you all."

Tane's grip tightened on his spear. "I have done no wrong. I fish only to feed my family."

The Taniwha's eyes glowed brighter, and the storm around them surged once again. "You speak of feeding your family, but what of the river? What of the forest? What of the creatures who depend on the waters for their lives? You are not the only ones who need these things, fisherman. The balance has been shattered, and I have been forced to act."

Tane felt a wave of realization wash over him. The Taniwha was not a force of destruction for its own sake. It was a guardian, a protector, and its actions were not born of malice, but of necessity. The storm had not been an attack—it was a desperate plea for the people to understand the price they had been ignoring for so long.

Tane lowered his spear, his heart heavy with understanding. "What do you ask of us, then?"

The Taniwha's gaze softened. "I ask that you restore balance. No longer shall you take without thought. Fish only what you need. Care for the river, care for the forests, and protect the creatures that call these lands home. If you can do this, the storm will end, and peace will return."

Tane nodded slowly. He could feel the weight of the Taniwha's words pressing down on him. The village had been blind, caught in its own desires, taking more than was needed and forgetting that nature itself required respect. It was not the Taniwha who was the villain, but the people's own greed.

"I will go back to the village," Tane said, his voice firm. "I will make them understand. We will change."

With that, the Taniwha's massive form began to sink back into the river, its great tail disappearing into the depths. The storm slowly began to fade, and the winds eased, leaving behind a strange calm. The dark clouds parted, and the sun began to shine once more.

Tane returned to the village, his mind racing with what he had learned. He gathered the villagers together, speaking to them not of a fearsome monster, but of a guardian that sought only to protect them and the land they relied on. Slowly, the villagers began to understand. They agreed to change, to fish only what was needed, to care for the river and the forests, and to live in harmony with the land.

In the years that followed, the village thrived in ways it never had before. The river flowed clearer, the fish returned in abundance, and the people lived with a newfound respect for the land and its creatures. The Taniwha, once a terrifying figure in their myths, became a symbol of the balance they had learned to cherish.

And Tane, the brave fisherman, never forgot the lesson of the Taniwha. It was not enough to simply take; one had to give back. The greatest treasure was not what could be taken from the land, but what could be shared with it.

The Taniwha's Mating Dance

In the village of Haerehua, nestled between verdant hills and a meandering river, there existed a tale as old as the land itself. It was the story of the Taniwha, a great and mysterious creature said to reside in the deep waters of the river that nourished the village. The Taniwha was not a mere beast but a guardian, a force of nature that influenced the very rhythms of the seasons. Yet, the villagers knew of it only in whispers, for the creature was as elusive as it was powerful. It was said that once a year, in the time of the great floods, the Taniwha would perform its mating dance—a sacred ritual that governed the fate of the village for the coming seasons.

The story of the dance had been passed down for generations, and it was said that the dance was a beautiful yet fearsome spectacle, a fusion of grace and power, whose outcome determined whether the village would thrive or face hardship. The mating dance was tied to the changing of the seasons, marking the transition from the rains of autumn to the warmth of summer. If the Taniwha danced with its mate, the river would swell, and the harvest would be bountiful. If it danced alone, however, the river would run dry, and famine would plague the village.

This ritual, this dance of life and death, was the heart of the village's understanding of the world. It was feared, revered, and always watched with bated breath. But no one, not even the eldest of the village elders, had ever seen it firsthand. The Taniwha, after all, was a creature of the deep, and though it was said to reveal itself in its most sacred moment, no human had ever been close enough to witness it. That is, until one fateful year.

Kai, a young man with an insatiable curiosity, had grown tired of the old stories and the endless speculation. His father was a fisherman, and his mother a weaver, both of whom had long obeyed the rhythm of the seasons dictated by the Taniwha's dance. But Kai, ever questioning, found himself at the edge of belief. "If the dance is so important," he thought, "then I will see it for myself."

So, on the eve of the sacred time when the river began to rise, Kai made his way down to the water's edge, determined to witness the ritual. The sky had darkened with the promise of rain, the clouds thick with the weight of the coming flood. The village was quiet in the stillness before the storm, as the villagers prepared for what was to come.

As Kai approached the river, the air grew thick with an odd energy, a hum in the air that seemed to vibrate deep in his chest. The water churned restlessly, as though something enormous moved beneath the surface. He crouched down, his heart racing, his breath shallow, and watched the water closely. His gaze shifted to the moon, rising high above the horizon, casting pale light over the turbulent river.

And then, he saw it.

At first, it was only a ripple, barely perceptible against the rest of the moving water. But soon, the surface of the river began to churn in earnest. The Taniwha emerged from the depths, its colossal body rising like a mountain from the water. It was magnificent—its scales gleamed like polished emeralds, and its long, serpentine form shimmered in the moonlight. Its eyes, glowing with an ancient fire, locked onto Kai with a piercing gaze that sent a shiver down his spine.

Kai froze, his pulse quickening, as the Taniwha began to move with a rhythm that was both mesmerizing and terrifying. The creature's movements were slow at first, like a dancer preparing for the grand spectacle, its body undulating through the water in a fluid, hypnotic motion. The very air around Kai seemed to pulse with energy as the river seemed to come alive with the creature's dance.

As the Taniwha swam gracefully in circles, a second form emerged from the depths—a mate, perhaps? This second creature was smaller, more delicate, yet equally as beautiful. The two Taniwhas circled one another, their movements a harmonious blend of grace and power, as though the very elements themselves bent to their will. Kai could feel the weight of the moment, the significance of the dance, but he also felt something else—a deep sadness that tugged at his heart.

The Taniwha's mate, its movements just as fluid, drifted farther from the larger creature. The rhythm of their dance began to falter, the syncopation broken, as if the Taniwha's partner was unsure. Then, suddenly, the dance came to an abrupt halt. The creatures parted, their bodies swaying in the currents, both looking toward the shore where Kai stood.

Kai held his breath, terrified and awestruck. What was happening? Why had the dance stopped? Had something gone wrong? Was the ritual failing?

As the creatures glided back into the deeper parts of the river, the moonlight illuminated the Taniwha's massive form, and for the first time, Kai saw the full weight of the creature's eyes—an ocean of sorrow, a world of ancient memories and broken promises. The Taniwha's gaze lingered on Kai, as if searching for something in him, something that had been missing for so long.

Then, the Taniwha's voice, low and sorrowful, filled Kai's mind.

"It is not the seasons that are broken, but the hearts of the people," the creature said, its voice like a distant rumble of thunder. "The dance of life requires balance, but the humans have lost their way. They have forgotten the true rhythm of the land and sea."

Kai's heart pounded in his chest as he understood the true meaning of the Taniwha's dance. The village had thrived when they lived in harmony with the world around them, when they respected the river's power and the land's gifts. But now, they had taken too much, and the river—the very lifeblood of the village—had begun to fade.

"I will return to them," Kai said, his voice trembling, but full of resolve. "I will teach them the dance they have forgotten."

The Taniwha's gaze softened, and with a final, graceful flick of its tail, it disappeared into the depths. The river calmed, the storm subsided, and the sky cleared, as though the world itself had been given another chance.

Kai returned to the village, not with the treasure of the Taniwha's dance, but with a new understanding. The lesson was not in the riches that could be plundered from nature, but in the balance that had always existed between the land and the people. He spoke to the villagers of the Taniwha's words, of the dance, and of how they must learn to live in harmony again.

And so, the seasons shifted, not because of the Taniwha's whims, but because the villagers had finally understood the true rhythm of life—the dance between humanity and nature, and how fragile that balance truly was.

The Taniwha's Mark

Lani had always felt different. Growing up in the quiet village of Koromiko, nestled between the sea and the forest, she had always been aware of the stories that surrounded her—a legacy of ancestors and the great Taniwha, the guardian of the waters. The village had its superstitions, its legends, and its warnings about the creatures that resided in the deep, but Lani had always dismissed them as nothing more than old tales.

That was, until the day the mark appeared.

It started small—just a faint, silvery line on her left wrist. At first, she thought it was some kind of rash, a mark from a thorn or a scrape. But over the course of a few days, the mark deepened, becoming more intricate, curling like a wave and radiating faint blue light. It wasn't long before her mother noticed it.

"What is that?" her mother asked, concern filling her voice as she gently traced the mark on Lani's skin.

Lani looked down at it, her heart racing. "I don't know. It wasn't there before."

Her mother paled, her hands trembling. "It's the mark of the Taniwha."

Lani recoiled. The Taniwha—wasn't that just a myth? A story told to children? But the look on her mother's face was serious, one that spoke of generations of inherited knowledge. Her mother quickly took her inside, drawing the curtains and locking the door.

"You must learn what it means," her mother said, her voice hushed and fearful. "The Taniwha's mark is a sign that you are no longer just human. You are its descendant. Its blood flows through you."

Lani's heart pounded in her chest. "But why me? I don't know anything about the Taniwha. I've never—"

Her mother's gaze turned solemn. "You don't need to know the old stories to understand the danger you face now. The mark... it is a gift and a curse. You must learn to control its power before it consumes you, before it drives you mad like the others who have come before you."

For the next few weeks, Lani found herself wrestling with the mark that now seemed to pulse with a life of its own. It burned at night, its glow becoming brighter, its shape shifting in strange ways that left her confused and frightened. She sought answers from the elders, but they only spoke in riddles, offering warnings rather than solutions. The power within her was ancient, and they had no knowledge of how to control it.

One night, after the mark flared with a violent intensity, Lani couldn't take it any longer. She ran out of the house, barefoot and wild with panic, toward the river that fed into the sea—the place where, as a child, she had heard the Taniwha's legend told most often. The river had always felt alive, and in her desperation, she thought that maybe it could help her understand the power growing within her.

As she approached the water, she felt it—the pull of the river, as though it called her by name. The air grew thick, and the water rippled unnaturally, swirling around her feet. She closed her eyes and allowed herself to fall into the sensation, the warmth of the water meeting her skin.

That's when it happened.

The mark on her wrist burned hotter than it ever had, and she cried out in pain as it seemed to writhe, expanding like an extension of her very being. A sudden surge of energy shot through her, and she stumbled back, falling to her knees by the riverbank. The world around her blurred, and then, through the haze, she saw it.

The Taniwha, its massive form coiling from the depths of the river, its eyes gleaming with ancient knowledge. It rose from the water, its body undulating gracefully but with terrifying power. Lani felt the

Taniwha's presence like an overwhelming force, both comforting and suffocating. It was not just a guardian; it was a part of her now, a being whose blood flowed in her veins.

"You are mine," the Taniwha's voice echoed in her mind, low and resonant, as though speaking from the depths of the earth itself. "I have waited for this day, for the one who will restore the balance."

The words made no sense. "Restore the balance? What do you mean?"

"You were born with this power, Lani," the Taniwha's voice was soft yet powerful. "I have given you the mark, but it comes at a cost. You are tied to me now. I have kept the land, the river, and the sea in balance for eons, but you, child, will carry that burden now. You must learn to wield the power I have granted you, or it will consume you."

The Taniwha's gaze locked with hers, and suddenly, Lani understood. She wasn't simply a descendant; she was the living embodiment of the Taniwha's power. The mark was not just a symbol—it was a key. And with it came not only great responsibility but also the potential for destruction. She could call upon the waters, manipulate the currents, but if she lost control, the river would turn against her, consuming everything in its path.

The Taniwha's voice faded, and the mark burned one last time before it went dark, leaving Lani gasping for air, trembling. She had seen the vision, felt the power, but she understood the truth now. She was part of something much larger than herself. The line between human and Taniwha had blurred, and the fate of the village now rested in her hands.

She stood slowly, her body still aching from the weight of what had just occurred. The river was calm again, but she knew it was only a temporary respite. In her veins flowed the power to create and destroy, a force that had shaped the very land she called home.

Returning to her village was the hardest part. Her mother had known all along what would happen, but how could Lani explain the truth? How could she tell them that their survival—and their destruction—rested on her ability to control the mark?

As she entered her home, her mother looked up with quiet understanding. There were no questions, only a quiet acceptance. Lani had been chosen, not by chance, but by fate. The Taniwha's power had always been a part of the village, but now it was hers to command.

But the lesson was clear: true power came not from domination, but from understanding the balance that power required. The river, the land, and the sea—everything had its place, and it was her role to ensure that nothing, not even the Taniwha's power, disrupted that delicate harmony.

She had the power to reshape the world. But would she choose to wield it, or would she let the river carry her away like so many others before her? The choice, as always, was hers.

The Taniwha's Dream

Zara had always been a dreamer. Since she was a child, her nights were filled with vivid visions—sometimes wonderful, sometimes unsettling, but always strange. It was as if her mind wandered to places far beyond the waking world, where the line between reality and imagination blurred. But lately, the dreams had become different, more intense, and far too real. And there was one recurring theme: water.

The first time it happened, she woke gasping for breath, her skin slick with sweat. In the dream, she had been standing on the edge of a great river, watching as the water churned and swirled in unnatural patterns. Something in the depths had stirred, something vast and powerful. And then, in the shadow of the waves, she saw it: a pair of glowing eyes, enormous and ancient, staring directly at her.

The eyes belonged to the Taniwha, the ancient water guardian that many believed had once protected the village of Te Ika, where Zara had grown up. The stories of the Taniwha had been passed down through generations, of a mighty serpent that dwelled in the river, its presence felt in the tides and storms that shaped the land. But Zara had always dismissed those tales as nothing more than folklore—until now.

The next night, the dream returned.

This time, the Taniwha spoke. Its voice, though silent, echoed in her mind like a thousand thunderclaps. "The river calls to you," it said. "There is danger in the flow. You must listen to the signs."

Zara awoke with her heart pounding, the words lingering in her mind like an unspoken command. What did the Taniwha mean? What danger? She had never paid much attention to the old legends, but she could no longer ignore the growing sense of urgency in her dreams. Something was wrong, something was coming, and it felt as if the Taniwha itself had chosen her to bear the burden of understanding its cryptic messages.

Over the next few nights, the dreams became more frequent. Each time, the Taniwha appeared in different forms: sometimes as the serpent in the water, sometimes as a swirling mist, but always with the same eyes—burning with the weight of a warning. The messages became more fragmented, a puzzle that Zara couldn't quite piece together. "The river has forgotten its path," one dream whispered. "The waters are restless; they will swallow all who dare approach."

Zara spent her days consumed by the dreams, the cryptic words tumbling in her mind like stones in a river. She had always been an inquisitive person, but the mystery of her dreams gnawed at her. The Taniwha's warning had to mean something—she had to understand it before it was too late. She began to study the river more closely, hoping to find a clue, an answer to the riddle in her mind.

One evening, as she sat by the river's edge, the water lapping gently at the shore, she noticed something unusual. The flow of the river, which had always been calm, was now turbulent. The waters were murky, swirling in strange patterns as though something unseen below the surface was pulling them in different directions. A cold chill swept through her, and she knew then that the Taniwha's warning was not just a dream—it was a reality.

Zara's thoughts raced. She needed to find out what was causing the disturbance in the river. The Taniwha had spoken of danger, and she couldn't ignore it any longer. As she watched the water, the swirling became more pronounced, and the surface of the river seemed to shimmer, as though reflecting a scene that wasn't there.

It was then that Zara saw it—the figure emerging from the water.

At first, she thought it was a trick of the light, a figment of her imagination. But no. The figure rose slowly, its form becoming clearer as it approached the shore. It was a man, tall and draped in a flowing robe made of water itself, his face obscured by shadows. The air around him crackled with a strange energy, the water still swirling beneath his feet.

"Who are you?" Zara called out, her voice trembling. She was not afraid, but the power in the air was palpable, and she could feel her heart race with the realization that this was no ordinary encounter.

The figure stepped closer, and Zara could finally make out his face—a face with eyes as ancient and deep as the river itself. It was the Taniwha. But it was not the serpent from her dreams; it was a man, a figure of the river, taking on a human form.

"I am the Taniwha," the man said, his voice resonating with the force of the river. "I have been waiting for you."

Zara's breath caught in her throat. The Taniwha? But how? She had only seen it in her dreams, never like this—never as a man.

"You have been chosen to understand the message I have sent," he continued. "The river is dying, and so is the land. But there is more to this than you know. You see, it is not just the water that is in danger. It is the balance of all things. The river has been neglected by your people, and now it is reacting—angry and restless. I am bound to it, and you... you are bound to me."

Zara's mind raced, trying to comprehend the enormity of what he was saying. "But how do I help? How do I restore the balance?"

The Taniwha's gaze softened, and for the first time, Zara saw the sadness in his eyes. "You must return to your people and tell them the truth. The river is not simply a source of life—it is a living thing, a reflection of their hearts and actions. If they do not change, if they do not learn to respect the balance once more, the river will swallow them whole."

Zara nodded, understanding finally dawning upon her. The danger the Taniwha spoke of was not external; it was the recklessness and ignorance of the people themselves. The river had become a mirror of their disregard for nature. The Taniwha had not just warned her of physical danger but had shown her the spiritual peril that awaited them all.

As the Taniwha began to fade, his form dissolving into the mist, he left Zara with one final message. "Tell them not to fear me. Fear the imbalance they have created."

Zara returned to her village, knowing that the Taniwha's message had to be shared, and that only through understanding and respect could the damage be undone. Her dreams had not only been warnings—they had been a call to action.

The lesson was clear. The Taniwha had never been an enemy to the village, but a reflection of its actions. And if they did not change, the river would consume them—not with rage, but with the silent erosion of disregard.

The Taniwha's Betrayal

For generations, the village of Te Tahi had flourished under the protection of the Taniwha. The river that wound through the village, winding its way from the mountains to the sea, was as much a part of their lives as the land beneath their feet. It brought fish to their nets, water to their crops, and a gentle rhythm to their daily lives. And always, just below the surface, the Taniwha watched over them.

The villagers spoke of the Taniwha with reverence, its great form gliding through the waters, its presence both feared and adored. It was the guardian of the river, the protector of the balance between the land and the sea. Each year, the village offered it tributes: fish, herbs, and a ceremonial feast, thanking the creature for its gifts and keeping the peace with the natural world.

But over time, as the village grew in wealth and numbers, something began to change. The once-respected rituals faded into routine, and the Taniwha's protection was taken for granted. The villagers became bolder, their greed growing as the seasons passed. They built larger boats, cast wider nets, and dug deeper into the earth for more land. The offerings became smaller, more hasty, and, eventually, stopped altogether. The Taniwha's protection, once a gift, was now seen as an entitlement.

Then, one fateful night, the unthinkable happened.

The villagers, driven by greed and the promise of riches, decided to divert the river's flow to irrigate more land. The great river, the lifeblood of the village and the Taniwha's domain, was changed—its course twisted to suit human desires. The villagers believed it would bring them more abundance, more power. They didn't realize the terrible cost of this action: the river's delicate balance had been shattered, and with it, the trust of the Taniwha.

That evening, as the last stone of the dam was set in place, a heavy silence fell over the village. The air grew still, and the sky darkened, as if the earth itself had taken a deep breath. Then, from the depths of the river, a rumble shook the ground, followed by a sound like the cracking of ancient stone. The villagers gathered on the riverbanks, their eyes wide with fear as the water began to swell.

From the heart of the river, the Taniwha emerged.

Its massive form rose from the depths like a mountain, its eyes glowing with the fury of a thousand storms. It was no longer the gentle protector the villagers had once known; it was a force of nature, a creature whose power had been betrayed. The Taniwha's voice, a deep, resonant growl, filled the air, and the river began to churn violently.

"Why have you done this?" the Taniwha asked, its voice echoing in their minds. "I have protected you, fed you, kept your village safe. And yet you repay me with betrayal."

The villagers stood frozen, their hearts heavy with guilt. It was too late to undo the damage they had done. The river had been diverted, the Taniwha's home had been scarred, and the balance that had kept them safe was broken. The weight of their actions was too great to ignore, but the fear of the Taniwha's wrath was stronger still.

The Taniwha's eyes glowed with ancient power, and for a moment, the villagers wondered if the creature would destroy them all. But as it loomed over the river, its anger palpable, something shifted in the air. A soft breeze swept through the village, and the Taniwha's gaze softened, just for a moment. It hesitated, as if torn between the desire for vengeance and the memory of its long years of protection.

"You have broken the bond between us," the Taniwha said, its voice quieter now, filled with an ancient sorrow. "I could take revenge—wipe your village from the earth and return the river to its rightful course. But I have always been bound by a greater law: the law of balance."

The villagers, their eyes wide with fear, waited for the creature to decide their fate. It was clear that they had lost the Taniwha's trust, but the question remained: would it destroy them for their betrayal?

The Taniwha's massive form began to sink back into the water, and for a moment, the villagers thought they were being spared. But the creature's voice, soft and heavy, reached them one last time.

"You have forgotten the most important truth," it said. "Without balance, nothing can survive. I will leave you, but the river will no longer flow as it did. The land you have taken will wither, and the sea will not bless you as it once did."

As the Taniwha disappeared into the depths, the waters calmed, but the air remained heavy with the creature's unspoken judgment. The villagers, stunned and fearful, returned to their homes. They had lost the Taniwha's protection, and though they tried to salvage the river, the damage had already been done. The crops began to fail, the fish became scarce, and the village, once prosperous, began to crumble.

Years passed, and the people of Te Tahi were forced to reckon with their betrayal. They rebuilt what they could, but the land never felt the same. The river no longer provided as it once had, and the harvests grew smaller with each passing season. The Taniwha's wrath had not been a fiery destruction—it had been the slow, inevitable consequence of breaking the natural balance.

One day, as an old woman sat by the river, watching the water flow quietly around the stone dam the villagers had built, she realized something. The Taniwha's choice had not been to destroy them, but to allow them to suffer the consequences of their own actions. The creature had given them the opportunity to learn. It was not revenge the Taniwha sought—it was restoration. And in that, the villagers understood the true lesson: balance is not something we can take for granted. It must be maintained, or nature will reclaim what was always hers.

The Taniwha's forgiveness had been the greatest lesson of all. And though the villagers would never see the creature again, they had learned to live in harmony with the land once more—no longer as masters of it, but as humble stewards, forever aware of the fragile balance that sustained them.

The Hidden Taniwha

The town of Haranui had always been defined by its closeness to the sea. Nestled against jagged cliffs with the vast expanse of the ocean stretching endlessly before it, Haranui's residents had learned long ago to respect the sea, its rhythms, and its many mysteries. But of all the stories passed down by their ancestors, there was one that stood out above the rest: the tale of the Taniwha, a creature said to dwell beneath the waves, guarding the balance between land and sea.

For generations, the people of Haranui had lived with the Taniwha's myth—a guardian of immense power who protected the village from storms and kept the waters calm, a creature both feared and revered. Some said the Taniwha could be seen in the early hours of the morning, its enormous form slipping through the waves before disappearing again into the depths. Others claimed that it was just a tale to keep children from wandering too far into the ocean's embrace.

But one thing was certain—the Taniwha had not been seen in living memory. The village, though coastal and thriving, had been spared from the worst of the storms that ravaged other towns, and no one ever doubted that the creature was still watching over them, hidden deep beneath the waters.

It wasn't until one summer evening that things began to change.

It started with the sea. The water, which had always been calm and predictable, began to grow restless. At first, it was a subtle shift—a few waves that seemed more forceful than usual, an occasional undercurrent that tugged at the shore with an unfamiliar intensity. Then, as the days passed, the water grew even more agitated, the seafoam churning as though it were alive. The fishermen, who knew the waters better than anyone, whispered among themselves. Something was different. Something had awakened.

One particularly windy afternoon, as a storm gathered on the horizon, a strange occurrence took place. A great rumble, like the sound of a distant thunderclap, echoed from deep beneath the ocean, shaking the land beneath the town. The waves rose higher, their movement erratic, like they were being pulled by an unseen force. And then, something remarkable happened—the cliffs along the coast began to crack, and a dark opening appeared, as if the earth itself was being torn apart.

Out of the blackened fissure came a cave, its mouth wide and beckoning. The waves receded momentarily, leaving the town in an eerie silence. The people stood frozen, staring at the opening in the cliffs, their minds racing to comprehend what they were witnessing. Could it be? Was this the hidden lair of the Taniwha, revealed at last?

Among the crowd stood Hana, a young woman whose curiosity had always led her to explore the boundaries of the village. She had heard the stories of the Taniwha all her life, had even imagined what it would be like to see the creature. She had never believed it was real, though. But now, with the sea in turmoil and the cave revealed, something inside her stirred—something that told her this was more than just another myth.

Ignoring the worried whispers of the villagers, Hana made her way toward the newly revealed cave, her heart pounding with a mixture of excitement and fear. The others, too scared to follow, stood back, watching from a distance as she approached the gaping mouth of the cave.

As Hana stepped inside, the air grew thick with salt and the scent of the ocean. The walls of the cave were slick with moisture, glistening like the skin of some ancient creature. The deeper she ventured, the louder the sounds of the sea grew, until it felt as though she were standing in the very heart of the ocean itself. The ground beneath her feet shifted, as if the cave was alive, and Hana's breath caught in her throat as the path before her widened into a vast chamber.

There, in the center of the cave, she saw it.

The Taniwha.

It wasn't the terrifying monster she had imagined. Its form was vast, but not monstrous. It was serpentine, covered in scales that shimmered like the ocean's surface under the moonlight. Its eyes, enormous and ancient, glowed with a soft, pulsating light. Its massive body was coiled gracefully, resting as though it had just awoken from a long slumber. Hana stood still, mesmerized by the creature's presence. It was both beautiful and haunting, its power evident in every ripple of its form.

The Taniwha's eyes met hers, and for a moment, the world seemed to stop. It was as if the creature could see deep into her soul, past her fears and doubts, understanding something about her that no one else could. In that instant, Hana felt a bond—a connection to the creature, to the sea, and to everything that had come before.

"You have come," a voice said, but not aloud. It echoed inside her mind, deep and resonant. "I have been waiting for someone to find me. For the time has come to restore the balance."

Hana's voice trembled as she replied, "But I don't understand. The village—why has the sea grown restless?"

The Taniwha shifted slightly, and the water within the cave swirled in response. "The people have forgotten their place. They have taken from the sea without respect, without understanding the power it holds. They have disturbed the balance I have kept for so long, and now they must face the consequences."

The realization hit Hana like a wave. The village had thrived because of the Taniwha's protection, but they had grown careless, taking the creature's gifts for granted. The sea had grown angry because the villagers had forgotten the sacred relationship between them and the ocean.

"What should I do?" Hana asked, her voice small.

The Taniwha's eyes softened. "You are the one who has awakened me. It is you who must restore the balance, not with force, but with understanding. Go back to your people. Show them the respect they have forgotten. Remind them of the ocean's power, and of the price that comes with taking."

Hana nodded, feeling the weight of the creature's words. As she turned to leave, the Taniwha's voice echoed in her mind once more.

"Do not fear the balance, child. Fear the destruction that comes from neglecting it."

When Hana emerged from the cave, the storm had passed. The sea had calmed, and the villagers, who had been watching from the shore, gathered around her in awe. She knew what she had to do.

The lesson was clear: the ocean, the Taniwha, and the land were not separate—they were interconnected, and the health of one depended on the respect shown to the other. It was a lesson the villagers had forgotten, but Hana would teach them once more.

And though the Taniwha disappeared back into the depths, its presence remained, a silent reminder of the balance that had been restored—not through fear, but through understanding.

Taniwha and the Earthquake

The tremors began at dawn, subtle at first, like the gentle rocking of a boat on the sea. But as the minutes passed, they grew stronger, more insistent, until the ground beneath the village of Te Pae began to shift violently. Buildings cracked and groaned, their wooden beams splintering like brittle bones, while the earth below churned like a living thing.

Amelia, a geologist from the city, had been studying the fault lines that ran through the region for years. She had always known that Te Pae sat on a delicate seam between two tectonic plates, but she had never anticipated the power of what was about to unfold. She had been in town visiting relatives when the quake struck, and now she stood at the edge of a crumbling cliff, watching as the ground fractured and split before her eyes.

"Not again," she muttered under her breath.

The elders of Te Pae had always warned of a time when the Taniwha would awaken from its slumber beneath the earth, but Amelia had dismissed it as myth. The Taniwha was a creature of the river, a force of nature, yes, but no more real to her than the stories of ancient gods and spirits that had shaped the landscape of this part of the world. Yet here she was, watching as the earth buckled and heaved, and a part of her wondered if the old stories had been more truth than fantasy.

She turned and began walking toward the village center, her heart pounding in her chest. Her mind raced, calculating the severity of the earthquake, estimating the risk of aftershocks. But even as her training took over, she couldn't shake the feeling that something much deeper was at work here.

As she entered the village, she found the local elder, Hemi, standing in front of the great stone circle that marked the boundary of Te Pae. His face was stern, his hands folded into the folds of his cloak, his gaze fixed on the distant hills where the shaking had begun.

"Hemi," Amelia called out, her voice strained with urgency. "What's happening? This isn't just an earthquake. Something's wrong."

Hemi turned to face her, his eyes wise but shadowed with a deep sorrow. "It's the Taniwha," he said quietly. "It stirs beneath the earth."

Amelia frowned, disbelief rising in her chest. "The Taniwha? That's just an old legend. There's no way a creature like that—"

Hemi raised his hand to silence her. "The Taniwha is no legend, child. It is as real as the land you walk upon. It has always been here, beneath us, deep in the earth and the waters. And now it is angry."

Amelia swallowed hard. She had heard the tales, of course—stories of the Taniwha's power, of its restless slumber and the toll it took on the land when it awoke. But she had never taken them seriously. Still, she couldn't deny the force that was shaking the village to its core. "How do we stop it?"

Hemi's gaze hardened. "We cannot stop it. But we may be able to soothe it."

Amelia felt a chill run down her spine. "Soothe it? How?"

"With respect," Hemi said. "The Taniwha is a guardian, not a destroyer. It is only angered when the balance is disturbed. You, as a geologist, understand the earth better than most. But you must understand that the earth is not just rock and stone. It is alive, a living being that feels the imbalance when it is pushed too far."

Amelia felt her skepticism waver. She had seen firsthand how the earth could behave in ways that science couldn't always explain, how the cracks in the earth could reflect something deeper than simple geology. But to think of the Taniwha as a living force, not just a mythic protector but an entity with emotions—she didn't know how to process that.

"How do we show respect?" she asked, her voice quiet.

Hemi motioned toward the hills where the shaking had started. "The Taniwha lies beneath the ancient riverbed, deep in the mountains. There is a place where the earth breathes. If we go there, if we make our offerings, perhaps it will listen."

Amelia wasn't sure what to expect. She had thought that science could solve everything—she had never considered that the old ways might still hold meaning in a world driven by technology. But she had no choice but to follow Hemi, for the village's survival seemed to hinge on something she didn't fully understand.

They climbed the hills together, the earth beneath their feet rumbling with each step. The air grew thick, charged with an energy that Amelia couldn't explain, and the further they went, the more it felt as though they were walking toward the heart of something immense, something ancient.

At the summit, they reached the riverbed, a place where the river once flowed but had long since dried up, leaving only a deep fissure in the earth. Hemi knelt beside the crack, his hands trembling as he pressed them against the jagged edges. "We must offer our humility to the Taniwha," he murmured, pulling from his cloak a handful of herbs and offerings. Amelia followed his lead, unsure but feeling a deep need to participate.

As they laid the offerings into the fissure, the ground began to tremble once more. The earth rumbled, but this time, it wasn't with anger—it was a low, deep vibration, like a sigh of relief. The Taniwha, it seemed, was listening.

Amelia closed her eyes, letting herself feel the pulse of the earth, a rhythmic thrum that echoed through her very bones. For the first time, she felt the land's heartbeat beneath her feet, a presence as old as time itself. And in that moment, she understood. The Taniwha wasn't just a creature—it was a force of nature, an integral part of the earth's balance. Its anger hadn't been directed at the village; it had been a response to the disruption of that balance.

As the rumbling ceased, a strange calm settled over the land. The ground beneath them stilled, the air cleared, and the world seemed to exhale.

Hemi stood and looked at Amelia, his eyes filled with gratitude. "The Taniwha has accepted our offering. It will rest now, and the village will be safe."

Amelia nodded, still in awe of what had just transpired. The earth had not been angry out of malice; it had simply been a reflection of the imbalance the people had caused. And in that moment, Amelia realized that some forces in the world couldn't be controlled—they had to be respected. Science alone couldn't explain everything. Some things were meant to be felt, not understood.

As they made their way back to the village, the ground beneath them steady once more, Amelia couldn't help but wonder how many times humanity had forgotten the deeper rhythms of the world, only to face the consequences of their disregard. The Taniwha's fury had been a reminder—not of power, but of respect. And in that lesson, there was a quiet wisdom that Amelia would carry with her always.

The Taniwha's Lullaby

The village of Rangi had always been cradled in the embrace of the mountains and the sea. For generations, the people there lived by a simple rule: respect the land, and the land would provide. It was a quiet village, with traditions passed down through families, and stories passed down through whispers. Among the oldest stories was the legend of the Taniwha, the river guardian that protected the people from harm. It was said that the creature's power could be summoned through a song—one passed down through the women of the village.

Ena had sung that song to her daughter since she was a baby, though she had never understood its true meaning. It was a lullaby, soothing and soft, meant to send a child into sleep with calm and comfort. "Hush now, my child, close your eyes," she would sing, her voice gentle and melodic. "The Taniwha watches, the river sighs." Her mother had sung it to her, and her grandmother before that. There was something sacred in it, something deep, though no one had ever explained why.

Ena had always felt a sense of peace when she sang it, a sense of connection to something ancient. She would sing the lullaby to her daughter, Mara, each night before sleep, the words flowing like a ritual, soothing the child's cries and filling the small room with warmth. Mara, barely two years old, would always fall asleep to the soft melody, her tiny chest rising and falling in peaceful slumber.

One evening, as the sun set behind the mountains, casting the village in hues of gold and purple, the wind shifted. It carried with it the scent of salt and something else—something ancient and unsettling. Ena stood by the window, her eyes narrowing as she watched the ocean's waves crash against the shore. The sky, once clear and calm, now seemed heavy, as if the air itself held its breath. The sea, always an unpredictable force, had begun to stir.

A rumble came from the earth, faint at first, like the far-off growl of thunder. It was strange—unlike the usual sounds of the wind or the waves. The trees rustled, and the ground beneath her feet trembled. It was as though the land itself was awakening, stretching, and she couldn't shake the feeling that something was drawing near.

She turned to her daughter, still lying in her crib, her small hands clutching the edge of her blanket as she gazed at the flickering light of the lantern. Ena didn't know why, but an urgent need to sing came over her. Perhaps it was the unease she felt in the air, perhaps it was the lullaby's power itself. She approached the crib, her voice soft as she began to sing.

"Hush now, my child, close your eyes,
The Taniwha watches, the river sighs.
The sea is calm, the earth is still,
Rest now, my love, the world stands still."

The melody seemed to fill the room, echoing off the wooden walls. As Ena sang, she felt a strange warmth in the air, as if the very song itself was reaching deep into the earth and the sky. It was as if the land itself was listening.

She continued to sing, the words flowing, soothing her daughter, but there was something different now. The room grew darker, the wind howling outside the small cottage. But the wind was not howling in fear; it was howling in response. The earth groaned beneath her feet, and in the distance, the sound of crashing waves became louder, stronger.

Suddenly, the door to the cottage slammed open, the wind gusting in with a force that nearly knocked Ena off her feet. She rushed to close it, her hands shaking, but then she heard something else—a sound from the sea, a low rumble that reverberated through her chest. It was no longer just the wind; it was the sound of something immense, something ancient.

At that moment, as if in response to the song she had been singing, the ground beneath her feet trembled violently. Ena's heart raced as the force of the tremors intensified. It was an earthquake—but unlike any she had ever felt before. The whole village seemed to shake as though it were being uprooted from its foundation.

Then, a vision came over her—a flash of a great serpent, its scales glistening like the moonlit sea. The Taniwha. The creature she had only ever heard about in stories. Her breath caught in her throat as she realized that the lullaby, the song that had been passed down through generations, was not just a soothing melody—it was a ritual. The song had always summoned the Taniwha's protection, and now, the creature had answered.

Outside, the waves grew higher, crashing violently against the rocks. But something strange was happening—the waves didn't reach the village. As though held back by an invisible force, the water seemed to stop just at the shore, where it foamed and surged but did not advance. The Taniwha, the river guardian, was holding back the fury of the sea, as it had done for centuries.

Ena's voice faltered as she sang the final lines of the lullaby:
"The Taniwha guards with a heart so true,
The earth, the sea, all is watched by you."

As the last note left her lips, the tremors ceased, and the wind died down. The air, thick with energy just moments before, settled into a strange, heavy silence. Outside, the sea returned to its natural rhythm, and the ground was still again. It was as though the world had never moved at all.

She stood there, frozen, unsure of what had just happened. The Taniwha had responded to her song, but not out of necessity. The Taniwha had always been there, protecting them—waiting for them to remember. All this time, the creature had been watching, listening for the call, for the lullaby that would summon it when needed.

And now, as she looked down at her daughter, Mara's eyes were closed in peaceful sleep, a soft smile on her face. Ena realized that the lullaby was more than just a song; it was a bond, a calling, a reminder of their connection to the earth, the sea, and the ancient forces that shaped their world.

The Taniwha's protection was never far away—it had always been there, waiting to be remembered.

The Taniwha's Waterfall

The village of Whakarua was perched on the edge of a breathtaking waterfall that cascaded down from the mountains into the shimmering river below. The locals called it Te Wahi o te Taniwha, the Place of the Taniwha, for it was said that the great river guardian, a Taniwha, dwelled deep within the waterfall's mist. The legends told of a creature whose eyes gleamed like emeralds, whose roar could shake the earth, and whose presence kept the balance between land and water.

To the villagers, Te Wahi o te Taniwha was sacred. They approached the falls with reverence, always careful not to disturb the delicate harmony of the place. The waterfall was not just a natural wonder, it was a protector, ensuring that the river remained healthy and the land fertile. No one dared take more than they needed from the land, and the waterfall was a reminder of that balance.

Then, one spring, a tourist named Jasper arrived in Whakarua. He was a photographer with an insatiable desire to capture the world's most beautiful places, not caring for the stories or the histories that came with them. His only goal was to make a name for himself, to sell photos of pristine, untouched landscapes to magazines and travel companies. When he heard of Te Wahi o te Taniwha, he couldn't resist. It was the perfect shot—a legendary waterfall surrounded by ancient stories. It would bring him fame.

Ignoring the warnings of the locals, Jasper ventured to the waterfall alone, armed with his camera and tripod. He climbed the rocks that bordered the falls, searching for the perfect angle, oblivious to the sacredness of the land he was trespassing on. He set up his equipment, framing the shot with the raging water tumbling behind him, catching the light of the setting sun. The mist rose like smoke, and the roar of the falls filled the air. It was magnificent, but Jasper was too consumed with his ambition to appreciate it.

He clicked the shutter, capturing the scene he had come for. But as the last frame clicked into place, a sudden chill swept through the air. The ground beneath his feet rumbled slightly, as if the earth itself had exhaled in discontent. Jasper looked around, unnerved but dismissive. It was just a tremor, nothing more. He quickly packed up his gear, eager to leave before nightfall.

But as he turned to leave, a deep, resonant growl filled the air, followed by a deafening roar. The waterfall seemed to tremble, its water surging with an unnatural force, as though something immense stirred beneath the surface. Jasper froze, his heart pounding. He turned, and through the mist, he saw it—two glowing eyes, brighter than the sun, staring back at him from the heart of the waterfall.

The Taniwha had awoken.

Jasper's blood ran cold as the massive form of the creature emerged from the water, its scales gleaming like polished stone, its tail thrashing through the river with terrifying strength. It was more magnificent, more terrifying than any story had described. Its roar shook the mountains, and the air around Jasper seemed to crackle with energy. The creature's gaze locked onto him, and he felt the weight of its fury.

"You have disturbed my home," the Taniwha's voice echoed in his mind, low and powerful, like thunder.

Jasper, paralyzed with fear, stumbled backward. "I... I didn't mean any harm. I just wanted a picture," he stammered, his voice barely audible over the roar of the falls.

The Taniwha's eyes narrowed, and the water around it swirled violently, pushing against the cliffs. "You have taken from me," it growled. "You have taken more than you know."

Jasper didn't understand. He hadn't stolen anything, had he? "I don't understand," he said, his voice shaky.

The Taniwha's presence grew more intense, its form rising higher from the waterfall, its body blocking the sky. The air was thick with the creature's power. "You have taken more than a photo," the Taniwha said. "You have taken my peace. You have disrupted the balance that has existed for centuries. The river, the land, the creatures—they are all intertwined, and you have broken that connection for your own gain."

Jasper's mind raced. The Taniwha wasn't angry about the photo itself; it was angry about the exploitation of the land, the disregard for the sacredness of the place. He had come here, ignoring the warnings, with the intention of profiting from something he didn't understand.

"I'm sorry," Jasper said, his voice barely more than a whisper. "I didn't mean to disrespect you. I didn't understand."

The Taniwha paused, its immense form looming above him. For a moment, the waterfall calmed, the roar subsiding to a low hum. The creature's gaze softened, and its voice, though still commanding, held a note of sadness. "I have protected this land for centuries," it said. "I have kept it in balance, but now, you and others like you seek to take, to consume, without understanding. You do not see the damage you cause, how the land and water are connected to the heart of everything here. The river is not just a resource to exploit—it is a living entity."

Jasper stood, trembling, as the weight of the Taniwha's words sank in. He had always seen the world through a lens of profit, of what could be captured and sold. But now, in the presence of this ancient creature, he saw the folly of his ways. The land, the water, the Taniwha—they were not just things to be photographed and sold. They were sacred, intertwined with the soul of the world.

"I understand now," Jasper said, his voice trembling with newfound humility. "I was wrong."

The Taniwha's eyes softened, and the river's violent current began to calm. "You may leave, but understand this: the balance is delicate. If you and those like you continue to take without giving back, the land will turn against you. The river will reclaim what was once its own."

With a final, deep roar, the Taniwha sank back into the waterfall, its massive form vanishing beneath the waves. The air grew still, and the mist settled back over the falls. The ground, once trembling with fury, now felt peaceful again.

Jasper stood frozen for a long moment, the weight of the creature's warning pressing down on him. He had come seeking fame, seeking profit, but he had left with something far more valuable: understanding. The world was not something to be consumed, but something to be respected.

As he walked back to the village, Jasper knew he would never look at the world the same way again. The Taniwha had shown him the power of balance, the importance of respecting the land, the water, and the stories of those who had come before him. And for the first time, he understood the true meaning of the phrase: "You can never take too much, or the land will take back."

The Taniwha's Love

Amira had always been drawn to the water. As a child, she would spend hours near the river, watching the ripples spread across the surface, feeling the cool breeze on her face as the sun dipped below the horizon. The village of Raukura was nestled at the base of the mountains, where the river ran deep and wild, carving its way through the valley before flowing out to the sea. But it was not just the beauty of the land that kept Amira close to the water—it was the stories. The stories of the Taniwha.

The elders spoke of the Taniwha as a creature of great power, a river guardian who had protected the land for centuries. Some said it was a great serpent that slid through the river's depths, while others claimed it was a spirit that could take on many forms. But Amira had always imagined it differently—a creature of both water and earth, neither fully one nor the other, caught between worlds, much like herself.

Amira's mother had often warned her not to venture too far along the river, especially near the cliffs where the waters were deepest. It was said that the Taniwha could be seen there, its great form emerging from the water in the quiet hours of the night. But Amira, now a young woman, had always felt a strange pull toward that very place. She was no stranger to the unknown, and the allure of the Taniwha's myth had only grown stronger with age.

One evening, when the moon was high and the village quiet, Amira decided to follow the river upstream to the cliffs. She had been hearing whispers from the wind and the water for weeks, a soft calling that tugged at her heart. The air felt charged with energy as she reached the edge of the cliffs, the river crashing below her, its waters swirling in a wild dance. She sat there for hours, the world fading away as she listened to the rhythm of the current, her thoughts wandering to the creature that lurked beneath the surface.

As midnight drew near, the river stilled. Amira's breath caught in her throat as a shadow moved beneath the water. The surface shimmered, and then, from the depths, a pair of glowing eyes surfaced. For a moment, she was frozen, unsure whether her mind was playing tricks on her. But the eyes were real, steady and unblinking, and they were fixed on her. Slowly, the water parted as the Taniwha rose, its massive form gliding through the river like a living mountain. It was beautiful—its scales glistened in the moonlight, and its body shimmered with an otherworldly glow.

Amira stood, her pulse quickening, and the creature's gaze seemed to soften, as though it recognized her. She was no longer afraid, but mesmerized, caught between awe and something deeper, something ancient. As the Taniwha emerged fully from the water, its head towering over her, a voice filled her mind.

"You have found me, child of the river."

Amira's heart raced, but she answered with a calmness she didn't quite understand. "I've heard the stories. I've always wondered if you were real."

The Taniwha's gaze deepened. "I am real, though I am not like you. I live between worlds, between water and land, between the earth and the sky. But you... you have always understood me, haven't you?"

Amira swallowed hard, her voice barely above a whisper. "I've always felt connected to the river, to the earth. I've always felt like I was meant for something more, but I've never known what."

The Taniwha's voice echoed in her mind again. "I, too, am alone in my existence. I watch the world from below, hidden from the eyes of humans. But I have waited for someone to see me, to understand me. And I believe you are the one."

Amira's breath caught in her chest. She knew it then—what had always felt like an unspoken yearning was something more. It wasn't just the river calling to her, it was the Taniwha itself. It was not a myth; it was a living being, and it had been waiting for her, just as she had been waiting for it.

As the creature lowered its massive head to her level, she reached out with trembling hands, brushing the scales along its neck. The sensation was electric, a spark of connection that coursed through her veins. She closed her eyes, allowing herself to sink into the moment, into the bond that was forming between them. It was as though the Taniwha had always been a part of her, as though it had existed in her blood and bones long before she ever knew it.

But even as the magic of their connection enveloped her, she knew there were things they could never share, boundaries they could never cross. The Taniwha, though powerful and beautiful, was not human. Its love was not a love that could be returned in the way she had always known love to be.

"You are not like me," the Taniwha said, its voice soft and deep. "You belong to the land of men. And I, to the waters."

Amira's heart clenched, the weight of that truth sinking in. "I know," she whispered. "But I will always understand you. Always."

The Taniwha's eyes softened, and it let out a low, rumbling sigh that echoed through the valley. "And I will always watch over you. From the river. From the earth. I will always be with you, even when you cannot see me."

Amira nodded, understanding now the true depth of the connection between them. It was not a love that could exist in the physical world, but it was a love that transcended boundaries. It was a love that existed in the spaces between moments, in the quiet connection between the land and the water, between the earth and the sky.

As the Taniwha slowly retreated back into the river, its form sinking beneath the surface, Amira stood at the cliff's edge, feeling both sorrow and peace. She knew that she could never be with the creature in the way she had imagined, but their bond would endure in her heart. And as the river flowed beneath her, she understood the lesson it had taught her: love is not always about possession, but about understanding and connection, no matter how distant or impossible it may seem.

The Taniwha was not just a creature of legend—it was a part of the world, and a part of her. And that, in its own way, was enough.

The Taniwha's Curse

The jungle had swallowed them whole, its dense, humid air thick with the smell of decay and the cries of unseen creatures. The group of adventurers, five in total, had trekked for days to reach the sacred river that was said to be the home of the Taniwha. They had heard the stories of the river guardian's immense power, the creature said to protect the waters and keep balance between the land and sea. The villagers in the nearby settlement had warned them of trespassing, speaking of a curse that would befall anyone who disturbed the sacred place. But the promise of treasure—the rumored treasure hidden in the depths of the river—had been too great to resist.

Lukas, the leader of the group, was the first to break the silence that had settled over the group as they approached the river's edge. His voice was low but filled with excitement. "We're almost there, I can feel it. This is the place. The Taniwha is real. And the treasure... it's just waiting to be claimed."

The others, a mix of hardened treasure hunters and thrill-seekers, exchanged uneasy glances. They had all heard the warnings from the villagers, but they had come this far, and there was no turning back now.

"Are you sure this is wise, Lukas?" asked Maeve, the quietest of the group, her hand resting on the hilt of her sword. "There's power in these waters. The Taniwha... it's no ordinary creature. If we disturb it—"

"It's just a myth," Lukas interrupted, brushing aside her concerns. "Stories to keep fools from taking what's theirs."

They stood at the edge of the river, the water dark and mysterious, flowing with a power that seemed to hum beneath the surface. The dense foliage around them grew thicker, and the sounds of the jungle grew quieter, as though the very land held its breath.

Lukas took the first step into the water, and the others followed reluctantly. The river was colder than they had anticipated, the current strong and unyielding. But they pressed on, their determination outweighing their growing unease.

As they ventured deeper, the air grew heavier, the jungle growing more silent with each step. Maeve couldn't shake the feeling that they were being watched, but Lukas pressed on, undeterred.

"I know the way," Lukas said, his voice confident, even though the path was treacherous. "The treasure lies just ahead. The Taniwha's lair is close. We'll be rich beyond our wildest dreams."

But as they reached the heart of the river, the water suddenly grew still. A deep rumbling sound reverberated through the ground beneath them, and the temperature dropped. The group froze, their eyes scanning the water, but it was too late.

The Taniwha rose from the depths, its enormous form breaking the surface with a force that sent waves crashing toward the shore. Its scales glistened in the dim light, and its eyes—green and glowing with ancient power—locked onto Lukas with a terrifying intensity. The creature's massive body coiled through the water, its movements graceful but filled with a silent menace.

"Foolish mortals," the Taniwha's voice echoed in their minds, a deep and resonant growl that seemed to come from everywhere and nowhere. "You have trespassed in sacred waters. You have disturbed the balance that has kept the land and sea in harmony for centuries."

Lukas stumbled back, his bravado crumbling as the weight of the creature's presence pressed down on him. "I—I didn't know," he stammered, his voice shaking. "We didn't mean any harm. We only wanted—"

"You wanted to take," the Taniwha interrupted, its voice cold and unforgiving. "And for that, you shall pay the price."

The water churned violently around them, and the Taniwha's massive tail slammed against the riverbank, sending the adventurers sprawling. The ground beneath them trembled as the river surged with fury, and the sky darkened, as though the very heavens themselves had been shaken.

"You have awakened the curse," the Taniwha intoned. "You will bear the consequences of your greed. The balance has been broken, and now you must suffer until it is restored."

The river calmed, but the curse had already begun to take hold. The adventurers could feel it—a creeping, gnawing sensation that filled their bodies with a cold dread. Lukas's hands began to tremble uncontrollably, his skin turning pale as the curse seeped into his bones. Maeve felt a sharp pain in her chest, and the others staggered, as though the weight of the curse was physically pressing down on them.

"What—what is this?" Lukas gasped, his voice strained with fear.

"The curse will consume you," the Taniwha's voice echoed, the threat hanging heavy in the air. "Until the balance is restored, until you learn the price of your actions, you will be trapped in this torment."

The adventurers tried to escape, to flee the river's edge, but it was too late. The curse had already claimed them. As they struggled to move, the river's pull grew stronger, dragging them back toward the water.

Maeve, her mind racing, remembered the old stories that the villagers had told—of how the Taniwha could only be appeased by restoring what had been taken, by offering something of great value to the creature. The lesson of respect, of balance, was clear now.

"We must give back," Maeve whispered, her voice trembling with the realization. "We've taken more than we deserve. We need to restore the balance."

Lukas, desperate to escape, looked at her with wild eyes. "How? How do we fix this?"

Maeve turned to the river, her heart heavy with the weight of their greed. "We must offer something in return. A sacrifice."

The Taniwha's eyes glowed brighter, sensing the shift in their understanding. "Yes. A sacrifice is the only way to end the curse. But you must give willingly. It cannot be forced."

The adventurers, now understanding the depth of their mistake, knelt by the riverbank, their hands pressed to the earth. With trembling hands, they removed the treasures they had taken—gems, gold, and relics—placing them back into the river.

"We offer this in exchange for the balance," Maeve said, her voice filled with remorse. "We understand now."

For a long moment, nothing happened. The water was still. The curse still gnawed at their bodies, but then, the Taniwha spoke once more, its voice softening.

"You have learned the price of greed. The curse is lifted, but remember this lesson: the earth, the river, the creatures that protect it—they are not for taking. They are for respecting."

The Taniwha's form receded back into the depths of the river, its eyes the last to disappear from sight. The water calmed, the air grew lighter, and the pressure that had weighed on the adventurers lifted.

As they made their way back to the village, their bodies sore but free from the curse, Maeve turned to Lukas, her voice steady but filled with quiet wisdom. "It's not just about the treasure. It's about the balance. We've learned that now."

Taniwha's Vow

In the village of Arahia, nestled at the foot of the mountains, the people lived in harmony with the land and the river that wound its way through their valley. For generations, they had told the story of the Taniwha, a mighty creature that guarded the river, watching over the village with a sacred vow to protect it from any threat. The creature, part serpent, part dragon, was said to have made a pact with the ancestors of the village, vowing that it would protect their land as long as the balance of nature was respected.

Oran, a young warrior of the village, had heard these stories all his life. He had grown up hearing the elders speak of the Taniwha's vow, of the creature's power and the deep bond it shared with the people. But despite his respect for the tales, Oran never quite believed in the creature's presence. He was a warrior, after all, trained to rely on his own strength and skill. But when news of invaders came to Arahia, Oran's doubts began to fade.

The invaders were ruthless. They came from the neighboring kingdom, driven by greed and hunger for land. They burned villages, took what they wanted, and left nothing but destruction in their wake. When they reached Arahia, the village leaders gathered to discuss what could be done to defend their home. But no one knew how to fight such an army, and fear spread like wildfire.

Oran stood before the elders, his sword at his side, his heart heavy with the weight of responsibility. "I will fight," he said, his voice firm. "I will protect this village, no matter what it takes."

The elders exchanged wary glances, knowing that Oran was brave but young. Still, they had no other choice. They agreed, but one elder, the oldest and wisest of them all, spoke a different kind of truth.

"You must first seek the Taniwha's blessing," she said. "Only with the creature's trust will you have a chance to protect this land. The Taniwha's vow is sacred. If you are worthy, it will lend you its strength. But if you are not, you will fail."

Oran's heart raced. He had heard the legends, of course, but he had never considered the idea that the Taniwha could be real—let alone that it might offer him aid. Still, he knew what he had to do. Without the Taniwha's blessing, Arahia would fall.

He set out alone, walking along the river that had given life to the village for as long as anyone could remember. The waters, usually calm and inviting, now seemed dark and forbidding. The trees whispered in the wind, and the sky overhead darkened with the promise of a storm. Oran's footsteps grew heavier with each passing moment, the weight of the task ahead settling deep in his chest.

Finally, after what felt like hours, Oran reached the sacred place where the Taniwha was said to reside. It was a secluded part of the river, where the waters churned violently, crashing against jagged rocks. The air was thick with mist, and the sound of rushing water filled his ears. Oran stood at the edge, staring into the depths, unsure of what to expect.

Suddenly, the river seemed to pause. The water stilled, as if holding its breath. Then, a low growl reverberated through the earth beneath his feet. A massive shadow emerged from the depths, and Oran's heart skipped a beat. The Taniwha rose before him, its enormous form coiling out of the river like a living mountain. Its scales shimmered with an otherworldly light, and its eyes—green and ancient—locked onto his with an intensity that seemed to pierce through to his very soul.

"You have come," the Taniwha's voice rumbled, not through sound, but through Oran's mind. "The time has come for you to prove your worth."

Oran swallowed hard, his throat dry. "I seek your blessing. The invaders have come to our village. We need your strength to protect us."

The Taniwha's gaze softened, but only slightly. "I have vowed to protect your people, but a vow is not given lightly. It must be earned, tested."

Oran nodded, understanding that the Taniwha's trust was not something to be taken for granted. "I will prove myself," he said, his voice steady. "What must I do?"

The Taniwha's massive head lowered, and the ground beneath Oran's feet began to tremble. "You must walk through the river's heart," the Taniwha said. "You must face the trials of the water and the land, to show that you understand both the power and the responsibility of protection."

Without warning, the waters around Oran began to rise, swirling in a violent maelstrom. The river, once calm, had transformed into a tumultuous force, pulling at him, testing his resolve. The Taniwha's eyes followed him, watching as he struggled against the current. Oran fought against the powerful waters, his body aching as the river tugged at him, threatening to pull him under. But he pressed forward, each step an act of will, his determination stronger than the pull of the water.

Finally, after what felt like an eternity, Oran emerged from the depths, gasping for air, his body drenched and exhausted. The river had tested him, but he had survived. The Taniwha's gaze softened, and it spoke again.

"You have proven your strength, warrior. But strength alone is not enough to protect. You must also have the wisdom to understand when to fight and when to yield. To protect the land, you must first protect the people's hearts. You must lead with honor, not pride."

Oran, still panting from the trial, nodded solemnly. He understood now—the Taniwha's strength was not just in its power, but in its wisdom, its ability to know when to act and when to wait.

"Go, warrior," the Taniwha said. "I will lend you my strength, but remember this lesson. The true power to protect comes not from the blade you carry, but from the heart that guides it."

As Oran made his way back to the village, the storm clouds above the river began to dissipate, and the land seemed to settle. The Taniwha's blessing had been given, and Oran's heart swelled with a new understanding of what it meant to be a protector. He was not merely a warrior—he was a guardian, entrusted with the care of his people and his land.

When the invaders arrived, they were met with more than just weapons. They were met with the wisdom of the land itself, and the strength of a heart that understood the true cost of protection. The invaders, unable to comprehend the power of the Taniwha's protection, were driven back, never to return.

And Oran, standing at the river's edge once more, realized that the greatest strength of all was the ability to listen, to learn, and to honor the land that had always protected him.

The Taniwha and the Ancient Tree

The village of Hinewai had always flourished under the protection of the Taniwha, a great river guardian bound by an ancient magic to an even older tree deep in the forest. The tree, known as the Kaikurā, was said to be as old as the land itself, its roots intertwined with the very soul of the earth. The Taniwha, a massive serpent with emerald scales that shimmered like the river's surface, had once been its protector and its prisoner. Bound by a spell cast by the village's ancestors, the Taniwha could not leave the tree's shadow, nor could it wander beyond the river's edge. But in return, the tree's magic gave the Taniwha unimaginable power, and for generations, the village had prospered under their guardianship.

For years, the villagers had lived in peace, their crops healthy, the river bountiful, and the storms kept at bay. But lately, a strange unease had begun to settle over the land. The river's waters were not as clear as they used to be, and the once-vibrant tree at the heart of the forest had begun to show signs of decay. Its leaves, once a deep green, were now yellowing, and its bark had started to crack and peel, as though something deep within the tree was rotting.

Lana, a young woman of the village, had grown up hearing stories of the Kaikurā and the Taniwha. She had always felt a deep connection to the land, and she had often ventured into the forest to visit the tree, knowing that it was the heart of their world. But now, as she stood before the ancient tree, she felt a coldness that made her heart race. Something was wrong.

The once-mighty tree seemed to groan as the wind swept through its gnarled branches. Lana placed her hand on its bark, feeling the tremor that ran through it. She could feel the life draining from the tree, the pulse of the land weakening. And then, from the shadows of the forest, she heard it—the sound of a deep, guttural growl, like the rumble of thunder.

The Taniwha emerged from the river, its great form sliding through the underbrush with a grace that belied its size. Its eyes, usually bright and full of life, were dull, clouded with something like despair. It moved slowly, its massive body coiling around the roots of the Kaikurā, but it did not seem to have the same energy it once had. It was as if the very magic that bound it to the tree had begun to fade.

Lana stepped back, her heart heavy with the realization of what was happening. The Taniwha was weakening, and with it, the protection it provided the village.

"You feel it too, don't you?" The Taniwha's voice echoed in her mind, a low rumble that sent a chill through her. "The balance is shifting. The tree's life is tied to mine, and as it fades, so do I."

Lana's voice trembled as she spoke. "What can we do? The tree is dying. The village is starting to feel the effects. The crops are failing, the river is turning muddy, and there is unrest among the people. How can we save it?"

The Taniwha's massive form shifted, its great tail sweeping the ground in frustration. "The spell that binds me to the tree was forged in ancient times. Only the power of the land itself can undo it. But it is a force that cannot be easily called upon. The magic of the tree is fading, and with it, so is the strength of the land. The village has taken too much from the earth, and now it must give back."

Lana's mind raced as she absorbed the Taniwha's words. The village had always relied on the land, but over the years, they had grown complacent. They had taken from the earth, harvested from the river, and built without thought for the balance. She had heard the old stories of the consequences of disturbing the natural world, but it had always seemed like something distant, something for the future. Now, the future had arrived.

"How can we give back?" Lana asked, desperate for a solution. "What must we do to save the tree and the village?"

The Taniwha's gaze softened. "You must restore the balance. The land must be healed, and the Kaikurā must be nourished. It is not enough to simply ask for salvation—you must prove that the people are willing to change. Only then can the magic of the tree be renewed."

Lana nodded, understanding the gravity of the task ahead. She turned and made her way back to the village, where the air was thick with fear and uncertainty. The people had gathered, their faces drawn with worry. They had felt the changes too, and the village was on the brink of panic.

"I know what we must do," Lana said, her voice clear and strong. "The Taniwha has told me that we must restore the balance. We have taken too much from the land, and now we must give back. We must rebuild our relationship with the earth. We must work together to heal the river, the forest, and the tree."

The villagers looked at her skeptically, but Lana's words rang with the truth of their situation. They had no choice but to listen.

Over the following weeks, the people of Hinewai set to work. They began clearing the river, removing the waste that had been left behind by years of careless harvesting. They planted new trees around the Kaikurā, nourishing the soil with care and respect. The village worked as one, restoring the land they had once taken for granted. They offered their own labor, their own sacrifices, knowing that it was the only way to heal what had been broken.

As the days passed, the Kaikurā began to change. Its leaves, once withered and dull, began to regain their color. The cracks in its bark began to heal, and a faint glow started to pulse within the tree. The Taniwha, too, began to regain its strength. Its scales shimmered again, and the power that had once flowed through the land seemed to return.

On the day that the tree fully bloomed once more, the Taniwha rose from the river with renewed power, its form glowing brightly in the sunlight. It coiled around the Kaikurā, its great body wrapping the tree in a protective embrace.

"You have done it," the Taniwha's voice echoed, full of pride. "You have restored the balance. The magic is strong again, and I will protect your village once more."

Lana stood at the edge of the river, watching the Taniwha and the tree, both brimming with vitality. She had seen firsthand how fragile the balance between the land and its people could be. The village had learned a painful lesson: that taking from the earth without thought would lead to destruction, but when the people gave back, the land would offer its strength in return.

The Taniwha's vow had been renewed, not through force, but through understanding and respect. And as the village flourished once again, Lana knew that the true power of the land was not in what it could provide, but in the way the people chose to live in harmony with it.

Taniwha of the Desert

In the heart of the Shifting Sands, a desert so vast it swallowed time itself, there lived a creature who had once ruled the seas. The Taniwha, a river guardian, had spent eons slithering through waters, its massive form cutting through the river currents like a force of nature. But centuries ago, the earth had changed. The rivers that had once flowed freely dried up, and the oceans themselves began to recede. In an age long past, the Taniwha had retreated into the desert, its once-pristine waters replaced by endless dunes and cracked earth.

The people of the desert knew the Taniwha's story, though no one alive had ever seen the creature. It was a tale told by the old wanderers, passed down through generations of those who trekked through the vast, unforgiving desert. The Taniwha, they said, had fallen into the earth when the seas fled, and it lay beneath the dunes, waiting for the day when the waters would return, and it would rise once more to protect the world.

Many who wandered into the Shifting Sands never returned. Some claimed the desert had swallowed them whole, while others said the Taniwha had taken them, its ancient wrath awakened by the intrusion of greedy souls. But to those who listened carefully to the desert's whispers, the Taniwha was not a monster—it was a guardian, a forgotten protector whose power was tied to the very earth itself.

Kaia, a young wanderer, had heard these stories since she was a child. Raised in the nomadic tribes that roamed the desert, she had always felt a connection to the ancient creature. She had spent her life studying the maps of the desert, learning the paths of the winds, and listening to the tales of the elders. But the story of the Taniwha fascinated her most—how the creature had once ruled the waters and now lay dormant beneath the sand.

One day, after years of hearing the tales, Kaia decided to venture into the heart of the desert to find the Taniwha's resting place. She had heard whispers of a sacred oasis, hidden deep within the dunes, where the creature's power was said to reside. Despite the warnings, she was determined to see the place with her own eyes. She set out, armed with nothing more than her courage and the ancient stories she had carried with her since childhood.

The desert was brutal, the sun unforgiving and the sand endless. Kaia had traveled for days, her skin scorched by the heat, her throat dry from the arid winds. The familiar songs of the desert filled her ears—the cry of the sand hawks, the hiss of the winds through the dunes—but there was something else in the air, something subtle and electric that Kaia couldn't explain.

As the sun began to set on the third day, Kaia stumbled upon a hidden canyon, a deep crack in the earth that seemed to draw her in. She could feel the air grow cooler, and the ground beneath her feet felt different—almost alive, as though the earth itself was breathing. She followed the canyon, her steps quickening as a sense of urgency filled her chest. In the distance, she saw something strange—a shimmer on the horizon, like a mirage, but it felt real, beckoning.

Kaia pushed forward, and as she neared the shimmering spot, she found herself standing at the edge of a vast oasis, an ancient body of water hidden deep within the desert. The water was dark and still, reflecting the sky like a mirror. But what caught Kaia's attention was not the water itself—it was the massive form that slumbered beneath its surface, half-submerged and coiled like a serpent, its body stretching across the length of the oasis. It was the Taniwha.

Its eyes were closed, but Kaia could feel its presence, an immense, ancient power that seemed to pulse with the rhythm of the earth. She knelt beside the water, unsure whether to disturb the creature or to leave it undisturbed. The air hummed with magic, and as she reached out a hand, she felt a connection, a thread between her and the creature, a bond that transcended time and space.

Suddenly, the Taniwha's eyes opened. They were not the vibrant green of a river guardian, but a dull amber, as though the life within it had long since faded. It stared at Kaia, and for a moment, the world seemed to stop. Kaia felt a flood of emotions—fear, awe, wonder—but also something else: a deep, aching sorrow. The Taniwha was no longer the vibrant force of nature it once had been. It was weak, its power tied to a world that had abandoned it.

"You seek me, child of the sands?" The Taniwha's voice resonated in Kaia's mind, a low rumble like distant thunder. "You have come to awaken the guardian. But you must understand—the power I once had is fading with the waters. The desert has taken them from me."

Kaia's heart raced. "I've heard the stories. The Taniwha was once a river guardian, but the seas disappeared. The desert claimed your strength, didn't it?"

The Taniwha's gaze softened, and it let out a long, mournful sigh. "The water is what sustains me. Without it, I am nothing more than a shadow, a memory of what once was. I guard the desert now, but I am not meant for it. The desert is too vast, too harsh. The river was my home. The world is out of balance."

Kaia understood now—the Taniwha's curse was not just physical. It was a curse of loneliness, of losing its purpose when the world around it changed. The creature was bound to an ancient duty, and without the river to protect, it had been left to rot beneath the desert sun, its power slowly fading.

"Is there no way to bring back the waters?" Kaia asked, her voice filled with desperation.

The Taniwha looked at her for a long moment, and Kaia could feel the weight of its ancient sorrow. "The world has moved on. The river is gone. The waters will not return, not in the way you dream. But you, child of the sands, you carry the memory of the river. You are connected to the earth, the wind, the water. If you understand that connection, you can help restore the balance, in a way I never could."

Kaia's heart clenched. The Taniwha was not asking her to restore the world to its past glory—it was asking her to find a new way, a way to make peace with the changes the land had undergone. "But I'm just one person. How can I do this?"

The Taniwha's amber eyes glowed softly. "You carry the wisdom of your ancestors. The balance is within you, as it is within all who walk this earth. The water may be gone, but the earth and the sky are still here. The desert does not have to be a curse. It is a new world, and you must learn to live in harmony with it."

As Kaia sat by the Taniwha, her mind racing with the weight of the task ahead, she realized the lesson she had been taught: The world would never be as it once was. But that did not mean it was lost. The balance between earth, water, and sky had shifted, and it was now up to her to guide others toward finding a new harmony. The Taniwha's sorrow had not been in the loss of its power, but in its inability to adapt to the changes it could not control. The real power was in the acceptance of transformation.

With a deep breath, Kaia made her vow. "I will carry the memory of the water with me. I will honor the river that was, and guide the people toward a new way of living, where the desert and the water are one."

And as the Taniwha slowly sank back into the oasis, its massive body curling around the depths once more, Kaia stood tall, ready to face the future, with the wisdom of the past guiding her every step.

The Taniwha's Gift

Eli was dying. The weight of his years had caught up with him, and the sickness that had ravaged his body for months now felt like a final sentence. His bones ached, his breath came in labored gasps, and every movement felt like the last struggle against an inevitable tide. The healer in the village had given up hope, and Eli's family had gathered around him, their faces etched with sorrow. It was a quiet death, one that came without ceremony or rage, just the slow, steady decline of a man who had lived too long.

The village was nestled near the river, a place where life was tied closely to the waters. Eli had known this river all his life, watched it as a child, learned to fish in its currents, and heard the stories of the Taniwha, the ancient water guardian. The creature was said to live in the depths of the river, watching over the land, protecting it from harm. Some said the Taniwha could grant wishes, others whispered of its great power, but Eli had always thought of the stories as little more than legends.

As he lay in his bed that evening, staring out at the moonlit river, a strange warmth filled the room. His eyes fluttered, and his breath slowed. The room seemed to grow stiller, the noises of the village outside faded, and the sound of the river grew louder, as though it were calling to him.

In that moment, Eli felt himself drifting away, his body no longer his own, his mind becoming detached from the pain. And then, in the space between sleep and wakefulness, he saw it—an enormous shape rising from the depths of the river, its form rippling with power. Its eyes glowed green, like emeralds in the moonlight, and its scales shimmered with an otherworldly light. It was the Taniwha, the great serpent of the river, but this time, it was not just a story. It was real, and it was looking directly at him.

"Eli," the Taniwha's voice boomed, though its mouth did not move. It spoke directly into his mind. "I have watched you all your life, as you have watched the river. I know your heart, your regrets, and your pain."

Eli felt a shiver run down his spine, not from fear but from an overwhelming sense of awe. "I—I don't understand," he thought, though the words seemed to form themselves in his mind.

The Taniwha's eyes softened, and it swam closer to the edge of his vision. "Your time is near, but I offer you a choice. A second chance at life, a gift, if you are willing to pay the price."

Eli's breath quickened. A second chance? The thought of living again, of feeling young and strong, was almost too much to bear. But then, a sense of caution swept over him. "What price? What do you want from me?"

The Taniwha paused, as if considering the question. "The river is the lifeblood of the land. It has sustained you, nourished you, and protected you. But it has been tainted. The balance has been broken. In exchange for your life, you must restore the river. You must bring the waters back to their true path and heal the land that has been poisoned by greed."

Eli's mind raced. The river had always been strong, its waters pure and vibrant. But in recent years, the currents had slowed, the fish had become scarce, and the land had begun to wither. He had seen the signs, but he had never known what to do about them. Now, here was a chance to fix it, to make things right—but what would it cost him?

"What must I do?" he asked, his voice barely a whisper.

The Taniwha's voice deepened, and Eli felt the weight of the creature's power. "You must give yourself to the river. Your life, your soul, will be bound to the waters. You will become part of the river, as I am, and you will guard it, protect it, for as long as it flows. But you will never again walk on land. You will never again be free of the river's depths."

Eli's heart clenched. He understood now. The price was not just his life—it was his freedom. He would become a part of the very river he had lived beside all these years, bound to it forever, never able to return to the world of men. His body would be lost, his humanity gone, and he would live as a guardian, a creature of the water.

But there was something else, something deep within him that knew this was the right choice. He had lived a long life, filled with regrets, missed opportunities, and broken promises. He had watched the world change around him, but he had never truly done anything to protect it. Here, at the end of his life, the Taniwha was offering him a chance to make a difference, to leave a mark on the world, to restore the balance he had neglected.

"I accept," he said, his voice steady, though his heart was heavy.

The Taniwha's eyes glowed brighter, and the river surged, its waters rising around him like a wave. "Then it is done."

In the instant that followed, Eli felt his body change. He felt himself dissolving, his flesh and bones becoming one with the water. The river rushed into him, filling him, merging with him until he was nothing more than a part of its current. The pain of his body's decay was gone, replaced by a strange sense of peace, of purpose. He could feel the river's flow, its pulse, its every bend and turn. He could feel the land's needs and the balance that had to be restored.

Eli no longer existed as a man, but his spirit remained with the river, watching over it, guiding it, protecting it. His essence flowed through the waters, and every time the river's current changed, he felt it in his soul. He had become the river, a part of something greater than himself, something eternal.

But as the years passed, Eli realized something he had not anticipated. The Taniwha's gift, though it had given him the chance to restore the balance, had taken away something more profound. He could no longer walk in the world of men, could no longer feel the warmth of the sun on his skin or the wind in his hair. He had traded his human life for a divine purpose, but at the cost of his freedom.

The river was indeed restored, its waters flowing with a renewed vitality, and the land around it began to heal. But as the river's guardian, Eli was trapped in an endless cycle, watching over the land he had once called home, yet never able to return to it. His gift had come with a hidden truth: that true restoration came at the cost of what one could never get back.

And so, as he drifted through the currents, Eli understood the lesson at last: sometimes, the greatest gift we can offer is not a second chance at life, but the acceptance of the price that must be paid for the world's healing.

Taniwha in the Mist

The small coastal village of Waiora had long been known for its beauty—its white sand beaches, towering cliffs, and the rolling waves of the sea that caressed its shores. But what the villagers knew best were the mists. They would roll in from the sea without warning, creeping in like an old friend, covering the village in a thick blanket of fog. The locals had learned to live with the mist. It was as much a part of their lives as the ocean itself, and they knew it as a sign that something ancient was near.

The villagers often spoke of the Taniwha, the great sea guardian who lived in the depths of the ocean. It was said that the Taniwha would rise from the mist to offer guidance to those who were brave enough to seek it. But only those with clear hearts and a pure vision could see beyond the fog and find the creature.

Mara had heard the stories her entire life, though she had always thought of them as nothing more than folk tales. She had grown up in the village, living a quiet, peaceful life. But lately, the feeling of restlessness had crept in, and she couldn't shake the sense that something was missing, that there was more to the world than she could see.

One morning, the mist came in thicker than usual. It was early, just before dawn, and the village was still quiet. Mara had been awake for hours, unable to sleep. She had a sense of unease, a feeling that something was on the verge of happening. When she stepped outside, the fog enveloped her instantly, and the familiar world became unrecognizable, replaced by shadows and swirling white.

The air was damp, and Mara felt the weight of the mist on her skin. She had always loved the fog, the way it made the world feel suspended in time. But today, it felt different. There was something alive in it, something watching. As she walked down the path that led to the cliffs, she heard a low, rumbling sound in the distance. The sea was unusually calm, but the sound was unmistakable. The Taniwha was near.

Mara's heart began to race as she reached the edge of the cliff. The mist seemed to part slightly, revealing a shape in the distance—something enormous and moving slowly toward her. She couldn't see it clearly, but she could feel its presence. It was as though the very air around her held its breath.

The shape emerged fully from the mist, and Mara gasped. The Taniwha was real—its massive body undulated like a serpent, its scales gleaming a deep, iridescent blue, reflecting the soft light of the fog. Its eyes were golden and ancient, filled with wisdom and sorrow. The creature's gaze met hers, and for a moment, Mara felt a deep, inexplicable connection. She had always thought of the Taniwha as a distant myth, but now it was here, alive before her, as though it had been waiting for her all along.

"You are brave to seek me out," the Taniwha's voice echoed in her mind, deep and resonant. "Most are too afraid to see beyond the fog."

Mara took a step back, her breath catching in her throat. "I... I didn't seek you. I didn't know... I mean, I didn't know I could..."

"You sought more than what your eyes could see," the Taniwha continued. "You felt the stirring in your heart, the desire for something deeper. That is why you have found me. I offer you guidance, but it comes at a cost."

Mara's mind spun. She had felt a pull, a restlessness that had led her here, but she hadn't expected this. The Taniwha was a creature of myth, of the sea, and it was speaking to her, offering her something she didn't fully understand.

"What cost?" she asked, her voice trembling.

The Taniwha's eyes softened, and for a brief moment, the world around Mara seemed to quiet. The waves were still, the fog paused in its dance. "To gain true vision, you must be willing to sacrifice the certainty of the world you know. To understand the unseen, you must let go of the fear of what you do not know. What you seek cannot be grasped with your hands, but only with your heart."

Mara's chest tightened. She had always been a practical woman, grounded in reality. But something in the Taniwha's voice stirred something deeper within her, something she had long buried. She had spent her life seeking answers outside herself—working in the village, trying to make sense of the world with logic and reason. But deep down, she had always known there was something more, something beyond the surface. And now, the Taniwha was offering her the chance to see it.

"I'm afraid," Mara admitted, her voice barely a whisper. "I'm afraid to let go of what I know. What if I can't handle the truth? What if it changes everything?"

The Taniwha's eyes shone with understanding. "The truth is not something to be feared. It is something to be embraced. Only by seeing with open eyes can you understand the world as it truly is. The mist hides not just the physical world, but your own heart as well. It blinds you to your deepest desires, to your truest self."

Mara closed her eyes, feeling the weight of the Taniwha's words. She had lived her life in the shadows of her own fears, never daring to step outside the life she had built, never questioning the things that held her back. But now, standing before the Taniwha, she felt the fog within her own heart beginning to lift.

"I will do it," she said, her voice strong. "I will see. Show me."

The Taniwha's form seemed to shimmer in the mist, and then, with a sudden surge of energy, the fog around Mara began to part. The world opened up before her in ways she had never imagined. Colors seemed more vibrant, sounds more vivid. The air tasted sweeter, and the earth beneath her feet felt alive. She could hear the whispers of the river, feel the pulse of the land beneath her skin, and she saw, truly saw, the interconnectedness of all things.

But there was something else—something deeper. In the distance, she could see the faces of the villagers, their lives entwined with hers. She saw their struggles, their dreams, and their fears. And she understood, with a clarity she had never known, that she was a part of something far greater than herself. The world was not just a series of isolated events—it was a living, breathing whole, and she was one small part of it.

The Taniwha's voice echoed again, softer now, as if it had been waiting for her to truly understand. "Now you see. You have embraced the truth. But remember, to see beyond the fog is to accept both the beauty and the pain of life. The vision is a gift, but it is not always easy to bear."

Mara nodded, feeling the weight of the Taniwha's words. She had seen beyond the fog, but she knew the journey ahead would not be simple. There would be moments of doubt, moments of fear, but she now understood that the truth was not something to shy away from—it was something to embrace, to live with, to let it guide her forward.

As the Taniwha began to retreat into the mist, its form dissolving into the swirling fog, Mara stood at the edge of the cliffs, her heart open and her vision clear. The world was not the same as it had been before, and neither was she. She had seen beyond the fog—and in doing so, had discovered herself.

The Taniwha's Lantern

The sea was always a dangerous place for those who didn't respect its moods, and for sailors like Gareth, there was a superstitious warning that had haunted them all their lives—the Taniwha's Lantern. The tale was familiar to anyone who made their living on the water. It spoke of a mysterious light that appeared on stormy nights, guiding ships lost in fog or tempest to safety. But the stories also told of a darker truth: the light was not a beacon of hope, but a trick, a lure sent by the Taniwha, a guardian spirit of the deep. Those who followed it, drawn by its false promise of refuge, never made it back to shore.

Gareth had heard the stories all his life, but like most sailors, he dismissed them as old legends meant to keep the inexperienced from venturing too far. After all, he had made a living on the sea for years. He'd sailed in every weather condition, every port, and he wasn't about to let an old myth send him running back to land. The sea was his domain, and he trusted only the wind, the waves, and his compass.

But tonight, the storm was unlike any he had ever experienced. The wind howled and the waves churned, threatening to tear his ship apart. His crew worked desperately to keep the vessel steady, but the elements were merciless. Just when Gareth thought they might finally breach the storm's edge, he saw it—a flickering light, hovering just ahead in the thick of the fog. It was a lantern, swinging gently in the wind, its glow steady despite the violent winds.

Gareth's first instinct was to ignore it. But then, a strange pull gripped him, as though the light was calling to him. The ship's wheel shuddered beneath his hands as the wind seemed to shift in its direction, guiding them straight toward the light. His heart pounded. It could be a lighthouse—perhaps a shipwrecked sailor had managed to light a lantern in the hope of rescue.

"Steer to it!" Gareth shouted, unable to shake the sense of urgency that gripped him.

The crew responded, though many of them exchanged uneasy glances. They had all heard the stories. But the storm was relentless, and the promise of safety, of refuge, was too tempting to ignore.

As they sailed closer, the lantern grew brighter, its light cutting through the fog like a beacon of hope. But the closer they came, the more strange the light seemed. It hovered, impossibly still, in the middle of the water, far from any shore. There were no rocks nearby, no land to speak of. Just the lantern, drifting like a phantom in the dark.

Gareth's instincts screamed at him to turn back, but his crew urged him forward. The mist seemed to thicken around them, swallowing the ship's sails and blinding them from the horizon. The ship groaned as if it too was reluctant to follow the light, but Gareth pressed on. His ship was caught in the spell of the lantern's glow, its pull irresistible.

It wasn't until the ship was almost directly under the light that the illusion began to unravel. The lantern's glow shifted unnaturally, pulsating like a heartbeat, growing brighter and then fading as though it were alive. And then, from the depths of the sea, a massive shape began to emerge. The Taniwha.

Its form was immense, a serpent-like creature rising slowly from the water, its scales glistening in the lantern's glow. The Taniwha's eyes were the color of the deepest ocean, and they fixed on Gareth with a terrible clarity. It opened its jaws, revealing rows of sharp, glistening teeth, its massive tail thrashing in the water as it rose higher.

"Turn back!" shouted one of the sailors, his voice full of terror, but it was too late. The ship's rudder locked, unable to steer, caught in the force of the Taniwha's presence. The lantern, now burning with a fiery intensity, seemed to beckon them into the creature's grasp.

Gareth stood frozen, staring at the Taniwha, unable to move, as if the light itself had paralyzed him. The creature's massive form towered over the ship, its voice deep and resonant, like the rumble of thunder.

"Why have you come, sailor?" the Taniwha asked, its voice echoing in Gareth's mind. "Did you think you could escape my depths, that you could take what is not yours?"

Gareth's mouth went dry. He had never believed in the creature, never thought the tales could be true. But now, staring into its eyes, he knew he had been wrong.

"We didn't know," Gareth stammered, trying to find his voice. "We thought it was a shipwreck, a distress signal."

The Taniwha's gaze softened for a moment, but then it shook its great head. "The light was never meant to guide you," it rumbled. "It was meant to test you, to see if you were wise enough to understand the dangers of greed. You sail these waters, taking what you desire, unaware of the cost."

The ship shuddered violently, as though it were being pulled into the very depths of the sea. Water began to pour over the sides, and the crew scrambled to secure the rigging. The lantern's glow became blinding, its light too intense to look at.

The Taniwha continued, its voice now filled with a quiet sadness. "You are like many who came before you, seeking a way out of the storm, unaware that the real storm lies within you. You follow the light, but you never see what lies beyond it. You take, you take, and you never give back."

A ripple of understanding passed through Gareth. He had sailed these waters, fished them, claimed them as his own. He had taken from the sea without thought, without respect, never considering the balance between taking and giving back.

"You wanted to be saved," the Taniwha said softly, its voice now almost a whisper. "But in seeking the light, you have overlooked the darkness within you. You did not ask for forgiveness. You did not ask for understanding."

Gareth looked around at his crew, their faces full of fear and regret. He knew the truth now. The Taniwha had given them the chance to turn back, to choose wisely, but they had followed the light blindly, thinking only of escape. Now, they had to face the consequences.

The lantern flickered one last time before extinguishing, leaving them in darkness. The ship lurched as the Taniwha's massive body retreated back into the depths, its form slowly sinking beneath the water. The mist began to clear, and the storm receded, but the damage had already been done.

The ship was battered, its crew shaken, but the true lesson had not yet fully taken root. The sea, the Taniwha's domain, was not something to be conquered or taken from. It was something to respect, something to coexist with. The light had not been a sign of salvation; it had been a test. And now, it was up to Gareth and his crew to return to the shore, not just with their lives, but with the understanding of the true price of their actions.

As the village came into view on the horizon, Gareth knew that the real challenge lay ahead—not in the storm they had survived, but in the choices they would make moving forward. Would they continue to follow the light blindly, or would they choose a path of respect and balance? The Taniwha's lantern had not just shown them the way—it had shown them who they were, and what they needed to become.

The Taniwha's Hoard

The salty wind whipped against Wren's face as the sun dipped lower in the sky, casting an orange hue over the churning sea. He had spent his life chasing myths, tracking whispers of riches buried beneath the waves, and now, after years of searching, he had finally found it—the Taniwha's hoard. Legends of the creature's treasures had long been spoken of in hushed tones by sailors and old fishermen, but few believed it. To them, it was another tall tale, the sort of story meant to scare children and fools.

But Wren wasn't a fool. He was a treasure hunter, and he had made a living from tracking down the impossible. The stories of the Taniwha's hoard had always intrigued him, and when he came across an ancient map in the back room of a forgotten tavern, he knew it was his destiny to find it. The map spoke of a sunken cavern somewhere off the coast of an uncharted island, and according to the legend, the Taniwha, an ancient sea creature, had hidden its vast collection of treasure there, beneath the waves, safe from the greed of men.

Now, standing on the deck of his small ship, Wren could almost taste the victory. His crew was anxious but eager, understanding the fortune that awaited them just below the surface. They had dived down several times already, but each attempt had yielded nothing but the cold, empty depths. Wren knew that the key to finding the treasure lay not just in the map, but in the very ocean itself. He had a sense for these things—an innate feeling that guided him like a sixth sense. And tonight, something told him the hoard was closer than ever before.

As darkness fell, the crew gathered their gear, preparing for another dive. Wren stood at the helm, watching the water, the surface now a dark mirror reflecting the stars above. The wind had died down, leaving the ocean unnaturally still, a glassy sheet that seemed to stretch endlessly into the horizon. For a moment, the world felt frozen in time, and Wren felt the unmistakable pull of something ancient, something watching, waiting beneath the surface.

"Ready?" Wren's voice was steady, but his pulse quickened with the anticipation of what was to come.

One by one, his crew lowered themselves into the water, their forms disappearing beneath the surface. Wren waited, watching the spot where they had descended, his heart racing in his chest. His eyes narrowed as the night seemed to grow darker still, the water taking on a strange, inky hue. Then, there it was—a flicker of movement, a faint glimmer beneath the waves, and the unmistakable gleam of something shining in the darkness. It was too far down for the lanterns to reach, but the faint reflection caught his eye.

"Down there," Wren whispered, almost to himself. "It's real."

Without waiting for further direction, Wren grabbed his diving gear and followed his crew's path into the depths. The cool water enveloped him, and he felt the familiar pressure of the ocean close around him as he descended. The darkness below was oppressive, yet he could still see the glimmer of something that shimmered like gold, glowing faintly in the abyss.

But the closer he got, the more unsettling the water felt. The pressure increased, and the temperature seemed to drop with every meter he sank. His heart pounded in his chest, and a voice in the back of his mind whispered that something was wrong—he wasn't supposed to be here. Still, his greed outweighed the warning in his gut, and he pressed forward, drawn to the source of the light.

Finally, after what seemed like an eternity, Wren's feet touched the ocean floor. He looked up and saw it—an enormous, hollowed-out rock formation, more like a cavern than anything he had imagined. And inside, nestled among the ancient, forgotten remains of shipwrecks, was the hoard—except, it was nothing like he had expected. There was no glittering gold, no jewels, no chests overflowing with treasures. Instead, the cavern was filled with a glowing, otherworldly light, illuminating hundreds of strange, translucent objects that seemed to pulse with a life of their own.

Wren moved closer, his mind racing. He reached out and touched one of the objects, feeling a strange warmth beneath his fingertips. It was smooth and firm, yet it seemed to shift slightly, like it was alive. When he pulled his hand back, he noticed the faintest trace of black ink starting to stain his fingers.

Confused, he took another look at the cavern. The shimmering objects weren't gold or jewels—they were bones. The remnants of creatures long dead, some of them human, others he couldn't identify. And now, they were glowing, their energy infused with something darker, something older.

A low rumble echoed through the water, and Wren froze, his blood running cold. The water around him began to churn, as though stirred by an unseen force. From the shadows, something emerged. It wasn't the sea creature he had imagined. It was something more terrifying. A great, serpent-like body, its scales shimmering like molten metal, but its face—its face was not one of power. It was one of sorrow. The Taniwha itself rose from the depths, its massive form coiling around the treasure hoard.

"You should not have come," the Taniwha's voice whispered in Wren's mind, its tone not one of anger, but of warning. "This hoard is not what you seek."

Wren tried to speak, but his words were lost in the deep. The Taniwha's presence pressed down on him like a weight, heavy and suffocating. Its eyes—deep pools of ocean green—studied him with an ancient, knowing gaze.

"What is this?" Wren's thoughts echoed in his head. "Where is the treasure? I don't understand."

The Taniwha sighed, the sound reverberating through the water. "This is the hoard," it said softly. "This is the cost of greed. The objects you see are the souls of those who came before you, drawn by the same desire. They followed the lantern's light, believing they could take what wasn't theirs."

The pieces of bone around them began to glow brighter, pulsing with a sickly energy. "This is not gold, this is not riches—it is a curse. A curse for those who seek to steal from the earth, from the depths, from the very soul of the ocean."

Wren's heart raced as the true nature of the hoard was revealed to him. His hands trembled as the black ink spread up his arm, a creeping, invasive stain that he couldn't scrub away. It was already too late.

"You've claimed your prize," the Taniwha said, its voice tinged with sadness. "And now, you too are bound to this place, to this curse. You will never leave."

The ocean around him seemed to pulse with energy as the darkness of the water engulfed him. The last thing Wren saw was the lantern's light, fading into the abyss, as the currents carried him away, bound forever to the treasure he had sought. The hoard was not gold—it was the cost of desire, the price of greed, and in the end, it was always the seeker who was claimed.

The Taniwha and the Lost Village

For years, the tale of the lost village beneath the sea had been whispered among the coastal tribes, a legend handed down from generation to generation. They spoke of a village once blessed by the Taniwha, a great sea guardian who had protected its people for centuries. The Taniwha's power was said to be tied to the village's prosperity, and when the waters rose and the village sank, it was as if the guardian had fallen into a deep, unshakable slumber, guarding the ruins from the prying eyes of those who might seek to disturb it.

But time, as it always does, eroded the truth. The stories faded, dismissed as nothing more than superstition. That was, until the archaeologists came.

Dr. Elara Meyers, the lead archaeologist on the expedition, had heard the rumors about the sunken village from her father, a marine geologist who had spent years studying the mysterious currents off the coast. Her father had always insisted that there was something hidden beneath the waves, something ancient and powerful, but Elara had never put much stock in folklore. Still, her curiosity was piqued when the satellite scans of the ocean floor revealed a large, unnatural structure buried beneath the sediment.

"It's there, Dr. Meyers," her assistant, Lucas, had said, excitement in his voice as he pointed to the data on the screen. "Right there. It matches the village location from the old texts. If we dive in, we might uncover something incredible."

And so, the expedition was launched. Elara's team, equipped with the latest technology, descended into the depths, eager to unlock the secrets of the past. They reached the site with ease, their submersible gliding through the dark waters like a silent ghost. The village, long forgotten by time, lay before them—its houses, streets, and even some of the stone carvings that had once decorated the village's temples, all preserved in the cold, dark ocean.

Elara couldn't help but feel awe as she peered out the window of the submersible. It was a perfect moment—history, perfectly frozen in time. But as they neared the heart of the village, something strange happened. The water, which had been calm and clear, began to swirl with unnatural intensity. The temperature dropped, and a deep, resonating hum vibrated through the submersible's hull.

"What's happening?" Lucas whispered, his voice tinged with concern. The team's equipment began to flicker as if the very fabric of the ocean was resisting their presence.

Then, from the depths, a shape emerged. It was colossal, a shadow moving through the water with an eerie, graceful power. Elara's breath caught in her throat as the outline of the creature became clear. It was the Taniwha, its massive, serpent-like body undulating in the water, its eyes glowing faintly with a sickly yellow light.

The sea guardian, which had once protected the village, had awoken.

"We shouldn't have come here," Elara muttered, her hands trembling as she gripped the controls. She had heard the stories about the Taniwha, but she had never truly believed them. Now, as the creature circled the village, its immense form blocking the light, she understood the depth of their mistake.

The Taniwha's eyes fixed on the submersible, its gaze a silent command. It moved closer, its body coiling around the submerged village like a protective barrier. The hum of the ocean grew louder, and the water around them seemed to thicken with pressure.

"This is bad," Lucas said, his voice panicked. "We've disturbed it. The stories—they were true. The Taniwha is real, and it's angry."

Elara's heart pounded. The ancient guardian was not just protecting the village—it was protecting the secrets buried within it. The Taniwha had slept for centuries, and now it was awake, its slumber disturbed by the modern world's unrelenting hunger for discovery.

As the submersible was caught in the Taniwha's gaze, Elara understood something profound—the creature had never meant to harm the village. It had been a protector, a force of balance between the land and the sea. The village had flourished because of the Taniwha's vigilance. But when the village had sunk, the Taniwha had been bound to the waters, never able to leave, never able to return to its place as guardian. Now, with the village disturbed by the adventurers, the balance had been upset, and the Taniwha was forced to defend what remained.

"What do we do?" Lucas asked, his voice trembling with fear.

Elara's mind raced. The Taniwha wasn't just a creature of myth—it was a force, a living embodiment of nature's wrath. There was no escape from its grasp.

"The village," she said, an idea forming. "We need to show it that we respect the land, that we understand its power. If we leave the village undisturbed, maybe it will let us go. We need to re-establish the balance."

But before she could give further instructions, the Taniwha's massive tail slammed against the submersible, sending a shockwave of force through the water. The lights flickered, and the submersible veered off course, spiraling into the depths. Panic erupted as the crew scrambled to regain control, but it was too late. The creature had made its warning clear.

Then, amidst the chaos, something unexpected happened. The Taniwha stopped. The hum of the ocean quieted, and the massive creature's eyes softened, glowing faintly as if it recognized something in Elara. She looked out the porthole, and for the first time, she saw something that made her stop—the reflection of the village, bathed in a soft golden light, its structure eerily intact.

The Taniwha wasn't angry at them, Elara realized. It was saddened. The village, its guardianship, had been severed, and in its absence, time had moved on. The people who had once lived there were long gone, their presence replaced by the greed and desire of those who came after. The treasure they sought wasn't gold—it was understanding, respect, and the realization that some things in the world were not meant to be uncovered. They were meant to be left in their rightful resting place, guarded by the forces that had kept them intact.

Elara took a deep breath, her voice steady as she spoke into the radio. "We've made a mistake," she said softly. "We will leave the village undisturbed. We will return to the surface, and we will leave this place to rest in peace."

The Taniwha's gaze softened further, and with a final, graceful movement, it drifted back into the depths. The water calmed, the pressure lifted, and Elara's submersible was no longer under threat. They slowly ascended back toward the surface, the underwater world now quiet and still.

As the team surfaced and breathed in the fresh air, Elara gazed out at the sea, the weight of their discovery settling in. Some treasures, she realized, were not meant to be found. Some things were meant to stay hidden, preserved by the balance of nature and the wisdom of time.

And the Taniwha, it seemed, had been its last guardian.

Taniwha and the Warlord

In the lands of Drenn, power was everything. Those who sought it did not hesitate to use force, treachery, or magic to seize what they believed was theirs by right. Of all the tyrants who had claimed dominion over the kingdoms, none were more feared than Warlord Saldrek. With a heart as cold as the steel of his blade, Saldrek had carved his empire from the bones of his enemies. He demanded loyalty through fear and crushed any who dared defy him. Yet even his iron rule was not enough to sate the endless hunger for power that gnawed at his soul.

Saldrek had heard the ancient tales—whispers passed down through the ages about the Taniwha, a creature of immense power that slumbered beneath the great river that flowed through the heart of the land. The Taniwha was said to be a guardian of nature's balance, capable of commanding the very waters themselves. But more tantalizing was the belief that the creature's strength could be harnessed, controlled by one who could earn its favor. Saldrek, ever the conqueror, decided that such a power would be the key to his ultimate domination.

He gathered his most loyal men and set off to find the Taniwha's resting place. For weeks, they traveled, battling harsh elements and fierce beasts, until they finally reached the river. The air around the waters was thick with ancient energy, and the village nearby had long been abandoned, as if the people had sensed the danger that lurked there. The villagers spoke in hushed tones about the creature, warning Saldrek that it was not to be provoked. But warnings meant nothing to a man like him. He had conquered kingdoms and slaughtered armies—what was one creature compared to the might of his will?

Saldrek's men built a platform over the river, and with great ceremony, they offered sacrifices to the Taniwha, calling out for its presence. Days passed, and still nothing appeared. Saldrek, growing impatient, ordered his men to dig deeper into the earth, convinced that the creature was merely hidden beneath the riverbed. The soldiers worked tirelessly, their pickaxes striking the ground as if they could force the ancient guardian into the open.

It was then that the river began to stir.

At first, it was a mere tremor in the water, like a ripple that spread too far. But soon, the waves began to churn with violent fury, sending waves crashing over the edges of the platform. The ground beneath them rumbled as if the earth itself was waking. Saldrek, with a greedy smile, stepped forward, his arms raised as if to claim the power for himself.

And then, from the depths, it emerged. The Taniwha, its enormous body coiling out of the river like a massive serpent, its eyes glowing with ancient fury. The scales of its body shimmered in the dim light, and its breath carried the weight of centuries. It was not the gentle protector that Saldrek had imagined, but a creature of wrath, its very presence a testament to the balance of nature that had long been disturbed.

"You dare to summon me?" the Taniwha's voice reverberated through the air, its voice a deep, rumbling force that shook the very foundations of the earth. "You who have disturbed the balance of the land, sought to bend the very river to your will?"

Saldrek, undeterred, stepped forward. "I seek power beyond your comprehension, Taniwha. Join me, and I will free you from this prison. Together, we will bring the world to its knees."

The Taniwha's eyes narrowed, and the river grew even more violent, as though the creature itself was angry at the very notion of being controlled. "You think you can control me, warlord?" the Taniwha snarled, its voice rising like a storm. "You think your arrogance can bind the river, the land, and the seas to your will? You are a mere speck in the face of the oceans. You are nothing."

Saldrek, his patience fraying, drew his sword, its blade gleaming with dark magic. "I am not nothing," he spat. "I am Saldrek, and I will not be denied. You will bow to me, or I will make you."

With a roar of defiance, he charged at the Taniwha, his sword raised high. But the creature, with a speed that defied its size, struck first. The water rose like a tidal wave, crashing against Saldrek and sending him sprawling across the platform. The force was overwhelming, and Saldrek's vision blurred as the river seemed to rise against him, a wave of power that he could neither fight nor control.

The Taniwha loomed over him, its gaze filled with ancient wisdom and unbridled fury. "You are nothing," it repeated, its voice like thunder. "You have not learned the cost of power, warlord. You cannot own the river. You cannot bend the earth to your will. Your greed has brought only destruction."

Saldrek, gasping for air, struggled to rise. His body was battered, his magic faltering in the face of the Taniwha's raw strength. He had underestimated the creature, and now he was paying the price.

But in that moment, something shifted within him. The pride that had fueled his ambition, the hunger for dominance that had blinded him, faltered in the face of the Taniwha's power. For the first time, Saldrek saw the truth of the creature's words—not as an obstacle to his rule, but as a force that protected the natural balance. His desire for control, his need to conquer everything, had led him to the brink of ruin. And now, facing the Taniwha's wrath, he understood that true power was not in domination, but in understanding, in coexistence.

"Spare me," Saldrek gasped, his voice broken. "I see now... I was wrong."

The Taniwha's gaze softened, its great form towering over him. The waves slowly calmed, and the fury that had filled the river receded. "You seek power, but you have not learned humility," the Taniwha said, its voice now quieter, less harsh. "There is no power in conquest alone, Saldrek. The land, the river, and the sea are not yours to command. They are a part of this world, just as you are. You must learn to respect the balance, or you will destroy what you seek to control."

The Taniwha did not strike the final blow. Instead, it receded into the river, disappearing into the depths with a final, regretful gaze. The waves returned to their calm state, and the platform beneath Saldrek was once again silent.

Defeated and broken, Saldrek stood in the silence. His sword, once a symbol of power, now lay heavy in his hand. He realized then that his ambition had cost him everything—his strength, his pride, and perhaps, his future. The Taniwha had not killed him, but had shown him the harsh lesson of balance: the cost of greed was destruction, not just for those around him, but for himself.

As the river flowed on, Saldrek dropped his sword into the water, the ripples spreading out into the horizon. He had learned too late that true power did not come from domination, but from understanding the land and its guardians. And so, the warlord walked away, his empire left behind, the Taniwha's fury lingering in his mind as a reminder of the price paid for ambition.

The Taniwha's Reflection

In the small coastal village of Makura, nestled between steep cliffs and endless seas, lived a man named Hemi. He was known for his strength, both physical and in character, or so he liked to believe. A fisherman by trade, he spent his days on the water, dragging in nets filled with fish for the market, always proud of how well he provided for his family. His wife, Miri, and their young daughter, Kiri, lived contentedly in their modest home. But despite the appearance of a life well-lived, Hemi harbored a deep, gnawing sense that something was missing. It wasn't hunger or need—he had plenty—but there was an emptiness, a quiet longing that lingered in the back of his mind.

One day, as a storm raged over the village, Hemi took to his boat, determined to catch the last of the day's catch before the winds grew too fierce. The waves were high, crashing against the sides of his small boat as the sky above darkened, and the wind howled like an animal in pain. But Hemi was undeterred; he believed his strength would see him through any storm. The waters, however, had other plans.

Just as the last of the daylight dimmed and the storm reached its peak, Hemi's boat was tossed by a massive wave. His nets, tangled in the chaos, snapped apart, and the boat was hurled against jagged rocks. The sea, always unpredictable, had finally claimed its due.

When Hemi awoke, the storm had passed, and he found himself washed ashore on an unfamiliar beach, his boat destroyed and his body bruised but alive. He staggered to his feet, disoriented, and as he took in his surroundings, something caught his eye. A figure stood in the distance, a person with their back to him, staring out toward the horizon.

He approached cautiously, unsure whether this figure was a survivor like him or some other unknown presence. As he drew nearer, the figure turned, and Hemi's breath caught in his throat.

The figure before him was human—no taller than Hemi, with long black hair and piercing eyes—but there was something strange about the way they moved. Their features were familiar, yet... not quite. A strange weight settled on Hemi's chest, as if he had seen this person before but couldn't place where or when. They smiled softly at him, an almost knowing expression.

"Lost?" the figure asked, their voice like a soft whisper of wind.

Hemi narrowed his eyes. "I don't know where I am," he said, his voice raspy from the storm.

The figure chuckled, a sound that seemed to carry across the waves. "You're on the shores of the Taniwha's domain," they said simply, as if that explained everything.

"The Taniwha?" Hemi asked, his mind still trying to make sense of the words. "But that's just a myth. A tale to scare children."

The figure smiled again, the same knowing smile. "Is it?"

Suddenly, Hemi felt a strange compulsion to look deeper at this person before him. As he did, a sudden clarity swept over him. The figure before him wasn't just a person—they were a reflection, but not of the world. It was as if the very air around them shimmered with energy, and in the eyes of the stranger, Hemi saw... himself. The Taniwha, it seemed, could shape its form into a human reflection, one that could see right through him.

Hemi stumbled backward, his heart racing. The stranger's smile remained, unperturbed by his shock.

"What are you?" Hemi whispered, suddenly unsure of whether the storm, or something far older, had taken his mind.

"I am the Taniwha," the figure said, their voice no longer gentle, but a deep, rumbling sound that echoed through the very earth beneath their feet. "And I am not just a protector of the waters. I guard the mirror that reflects the soul."

The air around Hemi grew heavy, as if the weight of the world itself had descended upon him. He swallowed hard, struggling to comprehend what was happening. "A mirror?"

"Yes," the Taniwha replied, its gaze penetrating. "A mirror to show you who you truly are, not the version you present to the world, but the one beneath. The version of you hidden even from your own eyes."

Hemi stood frozen, suddenly aware of the magnitude of what was happening. The Taniwha's voice shifted, becoming softer. "You have lived a life of strength, Hemi. Strength of body, strength of will. But you know as well as I do that your strength is not what you truly value. You may hold the world in your grasp, but you can't hold your own heart."

Hemi felt his pulse quicken. What was this creature saying? It wasn't just speaking to him—it was speaking into the deepest parts of his soul, parts of him he had long ignored, parts of him he had buried beneath his pride and his work.

"You've always given your strength to others," the Taniwha continued. "But when was the last time you gave something to yourself? To the love you have abandoned in your pursuit of what you thought was important?"

The world around him seemed to spin, and for the first time in years, Hemi felt vulnerable. He thought of Miri, his wife, and the years he had spent away from her, thinking only of providing, of surviving. He had been blind to her needs, to the quiet longing in her eyes when he returned each night, tired and distant. He had failed to see that the strength he used to push the world forward had, in fact, pushed away the one thing that truly mattered.

He opened his mouth to speak, but no words came. The Taniwha's gaze softened, its form rippling as if it was waiting for Hemi to accept what he knew deep down.

"Look at yourself," the Taniwha said, its voice a whisper now. "And decide. What do you truly value?"

Hemi's knees buckled, and he sank to the sand, the weight of the Taniwha's words pressing upon him. For the first time in his life, he saw the truth of his own reflection, the man who had become a stranger to his own heart. The power he had sought was not in the strength of his body, nor the weight of his work—it was in the connections he had neglected, the love he had taken for granted.

The Taniwha's form began to fade, its smile now a gentle, knowing one. "The journey forward is yours to choose. But remember, true strength comes from knowing what is worth the fight."

And with that, the Taniwha disappeared, leaving Hemi alone on the beach, the sand beneath his feet warm and familiar. For the first time, the world felt different—not because of the storm, but because Hemi had finally seen beyond the surface of his own life. He had glimpsed the truth hidden in his reflection—and for the first time, he knew what mattered most.

As he stood, the dawn light broke over the horizon. Hemi's heart was lighter now, and he knew that the real work had just begun—not to fight the world, but to rebuild the life he had almost lost.

The Taniwha's Mirror

The village of Aranui lay on the edge of a vast, storm-ravaged coastline, where the ocean was as wild as the stories that surrounded it. The villagers had always respected the sea, but they never dared to speak its true name. They referred to it simply as "the depths," where a creature both feared and revered was said to reside—The Taniwha. No one truly knew what the Taniwha was, but every fisherman, sailor, and old woman had a tale to tell about it. They spoke of a great beast that roamed the ocean depths, guarding a hidden power tied to the sea itself. And for generations, the Taniwha had never been seen. But some believed it watched over the village, a protector of sorts.

Among those who grew up listening to these stories was Leilani, a woman with a heart full of curiosity and a mind sharp as the cliffs that towered over the village. Leilani had always wondered about the Taniwha. It wasn't the stories of destruction that intrigued her; it was the sense of mystery that wrapped itself around the creature like a shroud. What if the Taniwha was more than a monster, more than a mythical force to be feared? What if it was something far older, something that held secrets no one had dared to uncover?

One evening, as Leilani wandered along the shoreline, her gaze fell upon an object half-buried in the sand. A glint of silver caught the fading sunlight, and she knelt to investigate. It was a mirror—old, framed in dark wood, and covered in intricate carvings. The mirror itself was polished but showed no reflection, only the deep shimmer of the sea's surface. There were no markings or inscriptions to suggest its origin, but it felt strangely familiar.

Leilani picked it up, feeling an unexpected weight in her hands, a sense of power contained within the simple frame. The mirror seemed to pulse slightly, as though it had a life of its own. When she held it close to her face, the reflection of the ocean began to shift. Instead of the sun-kissed waves and sandy shores, the mirror revealed something darker, something hidden beneath the surface.

In the glass, Leilani saw the Taniwha—not as a distant legend, but as a true presence. Its enormous form coiled within the depths, its green, shimmering eyes watching her through the reflection. But there was more. The mirror didn't just show the creature; it showed its true nature, its essence. Leilani saw the raw energy of the Taniwha, the ebb and flow of the ocean's power, connected to it, alive in it, coursing through the creature like a living force of nature.

But the Taniwha wasn't just a monster. It was more than that. In the reflection, Leilani saw something that stunned her—a flicker of humanity, of emotion, of yearning. The Taniwha was not a mindless beast; it was a guardian, a keeper of ancient secrets, bound to the sea by forces beyond comprehension. Its power was not one of destruction—it was a power of transformation, of balance.

The mirror began to glow, and a whisper reached Leilani's ears—soft, like the sound of the waves at night, but filled with power. "You see me now, child of the land," the voice rumbled, deep and timeless. "What you see in this mirror is not just my reflection, but your own. You, too, are tied to the sea. You, too, hold the power of the depths within you."

Leilani's heart raced as she stood frozen in place, the weight of the words sinking into her bones. Her connection to the sea—was that what had always drawn her to it? She had spent so much of her life gazing at the waves, longing for something beyond the village, something that could not be defined. Was this the answer she had been seeking?

The voice continued. "The power of the sea has been passed down through bloodlines, through those who understand the balance between the land and the water. But it has been forgotten, hidden away, and only a few have ever tapped into it."

"What is this power?" Leilani whispered, feeling both terrified and awed by the realization that she had been given a glimpse of something profound.

"It is the power to shape, to heal, to connect," the voice responded. "To understand the ebb and flow of life itself. The power to protect, as I do, and the power to destroy, should it be needed. You see, child, what you've always sought is already inside you. You have the gift of the sea, if you choose to awaken it."

The mirror's glow intensified, and the air around her seemed to vibrate with energy. Leilani felt a rush of warmth and cold, like the mingling of two opposing forces, swirling within her. The Taniwha's reflection began to shimmer, and Leilani realized she was no longer just gazing at it. She was *inside* it, feeling the currents of the ocean within herself, the pulse of the creature's power coursing through her veins.

A vision unfolded in her mind—a vision of the past, of ancient warriors and shamans, of a time when the balance of the sea and land was maintained by those who understood the deeper currents of nature. She saw how the Taniwha had protected the land and its people, how it had been a force for life, not destruction. And then, she saw how the power had been lost, forgotten by those who came after, who had failed to see the truth.

The vision faded, and Leilani found herself once again holding the mirror, now glowing with an inner light. She looked out toward the sea, knowing what she had to do. The Taniwha had not offered her power for the taking—it had offered her understanding, a connection to the forces that governed the world.

As she stood there, contemplating the choice that lay before her, she realized the truth. The power of the sea was not something that could be harnessed for selfish gain. It was something to be honored, something to be nurtured, something to be used only when balance demanded it. To wield such power was not a gift—it was a responsibility. And Leilani understood that now. The Taniwha had shown her the reflection not just of itself, but of herself, and in that mirror, she saw what she had always lacked: the wisdom to see beyond the surface, the courage to accept what lay beneath.

With a deep breath, she closed her eyes, offering a silent promise to the Taniwha, to the sea, and to herself. The power would not be hers to control. But it would be hers to protect, and in that, she would find her true purpose.

As the sun set on the horizon, Leilani turned and walked back toward the village. The Taniwha's reflection faded from the mirror, but its presence, its lesson, remained with her. She understood now—the deepest power came not from controlling the world around her, but from understanding it, from embracing the currents of life and trusting in the balance that connected all things.

Taniwha's Return

The village of Irihama had long been forgotten by the world. Once a thriving settlement nestled between steep cliffs and the sea, it had faded into legend as the waves swallowed its shores, its people, and its stories. For generations, no one had set foot in the village, and the world had moved on, as it always did. Yet, for all the years that passed, there remained whispers—a rumor among the elders, a flicker of a tale—that the Taniwha, the great sea serpent that had once protected the village, had never truly left. It had only slept, waiting for the time when it would rise again.

Kahu, a young fisherman from a neighboring town, had grown up hearing the stories. His grandmother, old and frail, had told him of the Taniwha's great power, of how it had watched over their ancestors, guiding them through storms and famine. But when the sea had claimed Irihama, the Taniwha had vanished, along with the people. The stories faded, and all that remained were ruins and the sea's relentless pulse.

Kahu's curiosity, however, had never waned. He often wondered if the old tales were true, or if they were nothing more than the fanciful imaginings of the old and the foolish. One day, driven by an irresistible urge, Kahu set out to find the village. He had no real reason beyond the yearning to see it for himself. The elders often spoke of a time when the village had flourished, a time before the great silence, but it was hard to believe that such a place had ever truly existed.

The journey was long and arduous, with the sea raging against him as if warning him to turn back. But Kahu was determined. The wind howled, and the waves rose higher with each passing day, but still, he pressed on. Finally, after days of struggle, he arrived at the edge of the long-forgotten village, its ancient ruins half-buried in sand, with the remains of houses and broken stone structures scattered like forgotten memories.

As Kahu stepped onto the soil of the village, something strange stirred in the air. The usual scent of salt and brine was mixed with a faint, earthy musk, a smell unlike anything he had ever known. It felt as though the very land had been waiting for him, as though it had been holding its breath for centuries, waiting for the Taniwha to return.

At the center of the village stood a stone circle, the remnants of a sacred site where the people of Irihama had once gathered to honor the sea. Kahu approached it cautiously, unsure of what to expect. The wind seemed to pause as he crossed the threshold of the circle, and the world fell into an eerie silence. It was then that he heard it—a deep, low rumble beneath the earth, a sound like the groan of something awakening from a long sleep.

The water surged, and the earth beneath Kahu's feet trembled. He stumbled, his heart racing, and turned to face the sea. The horizon was darkening, as if a storm was brewing, but it was more than that. The water began to churn, rising in great waves, and Kahu's breath caught in his throat as a massive form emerged from the depths, its scales gleaming in the waning light.

It was the Taniwha.

The creature had returned, its immense serpent-like body coiling up from the sea, its eyes glowing with an ancient fire. Its size dwarfed anything Kahu had ever imagined. The very sea seemed to bow to its power as the Taniwha rose, its head looming over the village like a force of nature, both terrifying and awe-inspiring.

Kahu stood frozen, the weight of history pressing down on him. The creature's gaze fixed on him, and for a moment, Kahu felt as if it could see into the very depths of his soul. There was no fear in its eyes, only a deep, ancient knowledge. It was not a monster to be feared—it was a guardian, an ancient protector whose power was far beyond the understanding of any mortal.

The Taniwha's voice, a low rumble, reverberated through the ground. "You who have come seeking the past," it said, "you stand at the edge of what was and what will be. The village you seek has been lost, as has the balance of the sea. But now, I return, as I have always returned, to restore what was broken."

Kahu's mind spun, his thoughts racing. "But the village is gone," he said, almost in disbelief. "It's just ruins. How can you restore it?"

The Taniwha's eyes softened, and for the first time, Kahu felt a flicker of something like sympathy. "The sea does not forget," it replied. "The people of Irihama were part of me, as I was part of them. They lived in harmony with the ocean, understanding that the tides flow not just in water, but in life itself. They took, but they also gave. In their greed, they lost the balance, and the sea took them."

Kahu's heart clenched with understanding. The stories he had heard, the ones he had always dismissed as mere legends, were true. The Taniwha had not just been a protector—it had been a keeper of balance. And the balance had been broken.

"But what about the people who are left?" Kahu asked, his voice trembling. "What do we do now?"

The Taniwha's gaze hardened, and the waves surged higher. "You must decide what you truly value, Kahu. The sea offers its gifts freely, but it demands respect in return. The people of Irihama took from the ocean without giving back, and they were lost. What will you offer in exchange for the sea's power?"

Kahu felt the weight of the creature's words. The land had suffered, and the sea had taken its toll. The Taniwha had returned not just to restore the past, but to challenge the present. The balance was still broken, and Kahu stood at the crossroads between redemption and ruin.

With a deep breath, Kahu made his choice. He stepped forward, his heart resolute. "I will give what I have," he said, "not to conquer, but to restore."

The Taniwha's eyes glowed brighter, and the sea calmed. "Then you have learned," it said, its voice now a soft murmur, like the ebb of the tide. "In giving, we find our place in the world. In taking, we are lost."

As the creature vanished back into the depths, the village stood silent once more. But Kahu knew, deep in his heart, that the return of the Taniwha was not just about restoring what had been. It was about forging a new path forward, one built on balance, respect, and understanding. And in that, the true gift of the sea was found—not in power, but in the wisdom to know when to take and when to give.

The Taniwha and the Rainmaker

In the village of Tapu, nestled at the edge of a parched desert, the land had long since fallen silent. The river, once full of life and teeming with fish, had dried to a trickle, and the crops, once abundant and lush, lay barren in the earth. The sky was cloudless, its vast expanse a pale blue canvas that seemed to mock the people below. For years, they had prayed, offered sacrifices, and done all that was asked of them, yet the rains refused to come.

In this desperate time, the village turned to their only hope—the rainmaker. Tui, a man of strange and ancient knowledge, was the last of his kind. He had been taught by the elders in his youth, learning the ways of the weather, how to call upon the spirits of the sky and earth to bring rain when it was needed most. For decades, Tui had been able to summon rain when it was most needed, but this time, nothing seemed to work. His prayers and rituals, once so potent, had been swallowed by the unyielding sun.

One day, as Tui stood on the barren earth, his mind desperate for a solution, a figure appeared at the edge of the village—a figure emerging from the misty shadows of the forest that bordered the land. It was not a man, but something far older, something immense and powerful, its form a fluid blend of shadow and substance. It was the Taniwha, the great guardian of the river, a creature of legend whose very name sent tremors through the village.

The Taniwha's massive eyes glowed with a deep, ancient wisdom, and its voice echoed in Tui's mind like a thunderclap. "I see you, rainmaker. You seek the rain, but you do not understand the cost. The balance has shifted, and the rains you desire may not come as you hope."

Tui, feeling the weight of the Taniwha's presence, took a cautious step forward. "I will do whatever it takes to bring the rain," he said, his voice barely above a whisper, the desperation clear in his words. "My people are dying. The land is dying. Please, help me."

The Taniwha's gaze softened, its enormous body shifting with a grace that belied its size. "You speak of rain as though it is a gift to be called at will. But rain is not a mere blessing—it is a force of nature, an agent of change. You cannot call it without consequences. If I help you, the rain will come, but it will bring with it more than what you expect."

Tui bowed his head, his hands trembling. "I understand. I only ask that you help us now."

The Taniwha stared down at him, its eyes glinting with the weight of millennia. "Very well, rainmaker. I will bring the rain. But know this: once it falls, there is no turning back."

With that, the Taniwha turned and slithered toward the horizon, its massive body vanishing into the distance. Tui stood still, unsure of what to expect, but he felt the air around him begin to stir. The wind began to shift, growing stronger and colder, and for the first time in years, a low rumble echoed from the sky. Clouds began to gather, dark and heavy, swirling above the land. The people of Tapu, who had long given up hope, stood in awe as the first drops of rain began to fall.

At first, the rain was gentle, like a soft sigh from the heavens. It soaked into the parched earth, bringing with it a wave of life that swept across the village. The crops began to perk up, the dry riverbed filled with water, and the villagers danced in the rain, their hearts light and full of hope. Tui stood at the center of it all, his face turned to the sky, his eyes closed in gratitude. But as the rain continued to fall, it grew heavier, faster, and more relentless.

The sky darkened further, and the rain became a torrent, sweeping through the streets like a flood. The river, once a dry creek bed, began to swell, its waters rising rapidly, threatening to consume the village. The rain fell harder and faster, the wind howling with a ferocity that seemed to tear at the very fabric of the earth.

Tui watched in horror as the village he had worked so hard to save was overwhelmed by the storm. The crops that had flourished only moments before were now submerged, the homes were flooded, and the once-barren river now raged with a power that seemed to have no end. He had asked for rain, but the Taniwha had given him something far beyond what he could have imagined. The very forces of nature had turned against him.

The Taniwha appeared once more, its massive form rising from the water, its eyes still glowing with that same ancient wisdom. "You have called upon the rain, rainmaker. And now you see its power."

Tui's heart was heavy with regret. "I didn't mean for this," he said, his voice breaking. "I only wanted to save my people. I never imagined the rain would bring such destruction."

The Taniwha's voice was calm, its tone almost compassionate. "The rain brings life, but it also brings change. The balance of nature cannot be controlled, not even by those who understand it best. What you see as destruction is simply the old order making way for the new. Life and death are intertwined. One cannot exist without the other."

Tui fell to his knees, the weight of his mistake crashing down on him. "What have I done?"

"You have seen the truth of what you asked for," the Taniwha said gently. "Sometimes, in our desire to fix what is broken, we unknowingly tip the scales. The rain, like life, is a force that cannot be contained. It will shape what it touches, and it will reshape you, just as it has reshaped this village."

Tui looked around him, the village now submerged in water, the people struggling to stay afloat. The crops were gone, the homes destroyed, but there was still hope. The Taniwha had brought the rain, and with it, the land would heal in time. The people would rebuild, but it would be a new beginning, not a return to the past. He understood then what the Taniwha had meant. Change was inevitable, and it was not for him to decide when or how it would come.

The rain slowly began to subside, and the waters that had flooded the village began to recede. The damage was done, but the land had been nourished. The people of Tapu would rebuild, and they would learn to live with the changes the storm had brought. Tui stood up, his heart heavy, but with a new understanding.

As the Taniwha turned to disappear once more into the depths, Tui whispered his thanks, knowing that the rain had been both a blessing and a lesson. In his quest to save his people, he had learned that sometimes, even the greatest forces of nature could not be controlled. But in their wake, there was always the possibility of renewal, of new life—if one had the courage to embrace it.

Taniwha's Blessing

The village of Hākau sat at the edge of the great river, where the waters whispered ancient secrets and the land was fertile, always bursting with life. For generations, the villagers had lived in harmony with the river and the Taniwha, the great creature who was said to dwell beneath its depths. The Taniwha was more than just a guardian; it was a protector, a force that kept the river in balance, ensuring that the seasons changed, the crops grew, and the fish swam freely. It was said that the Taniwha blessed the land, and those who were favored by it lived prosperous, if sometimes strange, lives.

It was on the night of the full moon that Mara gave birth to her child. The sky was clear, and the river sparkled beneath the stars. There was no warning, no sign of trouble when the waters suddenly surged and rippled in a way that was unlike anything the villagers had seen before. When Mara's child, a boy she named Ikaika, was born, there was a strange calm that followed, as if the river itself had held its breath. The moment the child's cry broke the stillness, the water receded, and the land seemed to breathe again.

The villagers, seeing this miracle, believed that Ikaika was blessed by the Taniwha itself, for no child had ever been born under such mysterious circumstances. His arrival was marked by the river's strange behavior, and for that reason, they treated him with reverence. However, as Ikaika grew, the blessings of the Taniwha did not come without a price.

From an early age, Ikaika showed signs of extraordinary abilities, but they were not the kind of gifts that most people would envy. He could call the rain with a whisper, and the fish would swim toward him as though drawn by an invisible current. He could make the plants grow faster, and he often heard the whispers of the river in his dreams. But for every blessing, there was a challenge. The rains he called would often come too swiftly, flooding the fields with water that ruined the harvest. The fish, though abundant, would sometimes vanish without warning, leaving the village hungry for days. The plants that grew too quickly often became overgrown, tangled in a chaotic mess that no one could untangle. Ikaika was both a blessing and a curse to his people.

As he grew older, Ikaika struggled with the strange duality of his life. He could not understand why the Taniwha, who had blessed him, had also given him such burdens. Why could he control the rain but not its consequences? Why could he hear the river speak but not understand the language it used? These questions tormented him as he grew into a young man, and the villagers, though grateful for his gifts, began to fear the consequences of his presence. Whispers spread that the Taniwha's blessing was not as it seemed, that Ikaika was too powerful for his own good.

One evening, after another inexplicable storm had ravaged the village, Ikaika went to the river, seeking answers. He stood on the riverbank, staring at the still water, his heart heavy with frustration. "Why have you given me these gifts if they only bring harm?" he called out into the night, his voice trembling with emotion. "What is your purpose? What am I to do with this power?"

The waters stirred in response, and from the depths, a great shape emerged. The Taniwha rose from the river with an elegance that took Ikaika's breath away. Its massive, serpentine form shimmered in the moonlight, and its eyes gleamed with ancient wisdom. "You have asked the right question, child of the river," the Taniwha's voice echoed in Ikaika's mind, a deep, rumbling sound that resonated through his bones.

"I didn't ask for this," Ikaika replied, his voice filled with both wonder and frustration. "I never asked for these powers. I only want to understand why they come with such pain."

The Taniwha's eyes softened, and the river stilled. "You have always been a part of the river, Ikaika. Your birth, your life—it is intertwined with the currents that flow beneath the surface. The rain, the growth, the abundance—they are but reflections of the balance of nature. You are a part of that balance, but you are also a part of its chaos."

Ikaika's heart clenched. "I don't understand. I thought I was chosen to bring harmony, to help. But all I've done is cause turmoil."

The Taniwha's gaze deepened. "The river does not flow in a straight line. It twists, it turns, it carves paths through the land. It does not always bring what is expected, but it always brings what is needed. Your powers, though they seem uncontrollable, are a part of the natural order. You are not meant to control them, but to learn to live with them, just as the river learns to flow around the obstacles in its path."

Ikaika closed his eyes, the weight of the Taniwha's words settling in his heart. "So, I am not meant to change the world? I am meant to live with it as it is?"

"Yes," the Taniwha answered. "You must learn to accept that both the blessings and the challenges are part of the same current. The rain you call may come in torrents, but it nourishes the land as much as it overwhelms it. The fish that flee from you may return when the balance shifts. And the plants that grow too fast may be a reminder to slow down, to understand that growth cannot always be rushed. You must learn to live with the consequences, to see that they are not punishments, but lessons in the balance of life."

Ikaika stood in silence, the weight of the Taniwha's words sinking into his soul. He had spent so much of his life trying to control the flow of his gifts, trying to impose his will on the world around him. But in doing so, he had missed the deeper truth—the balance was not something to be controlled; it was something to be understood.

"I see now," Ikaika said quietly, his voice steady. "I am a part of the river, and the river is a part of me. I must not fear the consequences, but embrace them as part of the flow."

The Taniwha nodded, its massive form shifting with a grace that seemed to ripple the very air. "You are beginning to understand. Now, you must live with the balance, not as its master, but as its student. And in that, you will find peace."

As the Taniwha sank back into the river, its great body disappearing beneath the water, Ikaika felt a calm settle within him. For the first time, he understood. The power he had been given was not a burden to carry—it was a gift to be embraced, with all its chaos and beauty. And as the river flowed on, so too would his life, intertwined with the forces of nature, guided by the wisdom of the Taniwha's blessing.

The Taniwha's Embrace

Liam had been at sea for months, a sailor on a merchant ship bound for ports he had never seen, a life of hard work and harder winds. The sea had always been both a lover and a tormentor—one minute, serene and beautiful, the next, merciless and wild. The storm came out of nowhere, fierce and violent, ripping the sails and throwing the ship like a toy in a child's hands. He remembered the sound of splintering wood, the rush of water, and then—nothing.

When Liam opened his eyes again, the sea had calmed, and the storm was just a memory. His body ached, and his mouth was dry. He coughed up seawater, struggling to push himself up, but found his arms too weak. His head spun as he lay on the shore, the sun casting golden light across the smooth sand. There were no sounds of birds or the usual bustling life of the sea. It was as though the world itself had fallen silent.

When his vision cleared, he saw a figure emerging from the water—a shape so immense that it seemed to dwarf the very horizon. At first, he thought it was some hallucination, the product of the saltwater and exhaustion. But then, the figure drew closer, and he saw the long, serpentine form of a creature—a giant, its scales shimmering like polished emeralds. The Taniwha.

Liam had heard the legends, of course—every sailor knew the stories of the Taniwha, the mighty sea guardian that was said to protect the waters and the creatures within. Some said the Taniwha could heal the wounded, others that it could bring terrible storms or sink entire fleets. But he never thought he would encounter one. Certainly not like this.

The creature's gaze met his, and a strange warmth radiated through him. It was not the cold, distant gaze of a beast, but the knowing look of something ancient, wise, and protective. He tried to move, but his body refused to obey. The Taniwha reached out, its enormous body coiling gently around him, lifting him with surprising tenderness. Despite the creature's size, it felt as though the very ocean itself was cradling him.

"Fear not, sailor," a voice echoed inside his mind, smooth and deep as the ocean's depths. "You have been saved, but the sea has its own way of binding those it touches."

Liam tried to speak, but his throat was raw, and his words failed him. His heart raced, part from fear, part from awe. How could this be real? How was he hearing the creature's voice in his head? But there was no denying it—the Taniwha, in all its power, had spared his life. The sea had chosen him.

He passed out before he could form another thought.

When he awoke again, it was to the sound of water gently lapping against the shore and the rustling of leaves in the breeze. He was lying on soft grass beneath a canopy of trees, the world still and peaceful. The air smelled of salt and earth, the tang of the ocean mixing with the scent of damp foliage. He tried to sit up but found his body still weak, his muscles sore from the ordeal. Yet, he felt stronger somehow, as though something inside him had been reset.

"You are awake," the voice came again, and Liam turned to see the Taniwha's head looming just above the waterline. Its eyes were focused on him, calm and steady. "I have brought you here to recover, but you must understand, sailor, that your life is now entwined with mine."

Liam's heart skipped a beat. "Entwined? How?"

"You were saved, but my power has also seeped into you," the Taniwha explained. "You are no longer just a sailor. You are part of the sea now, part of the currents that flow beneath the surface."

Liam blinked, trying to process the words. "I don't understand. How could I be part of the sea? I'm just a man."

The Taniwha's eyes softened. "You are not just a man, Liam. You have been chosen. The sea has seen your soul, your resilience, and your heart. But there is a cost. The storm that brought you here was no accident. Your ship was not the only one caught in it. Many others were lost, their fates sealed in the same way."

Liam's stomach turned. "You mean... my shipmates?"

The Taniwha nodded slowly. "Yes. But now, you must decide what kind of man you will be. The sea is vast, and its power is great. But it is not without its consequences."

Liam thought of his lost crew, his friends who had sailed alongside him for years. They were gone now, their lives taken by the storm that had ravaged them. And yet, here he was, alive—saved by the very force that had doomed them.

"I don't want to be part of the sea," Liam said, his voice thick with regret and confusion. "I want to go home. I want to return to land."

The Taniwha's gaze deepened. "You can never return to what you once were, Liam. The sea has marked you, as it has marked so many before you. Once touched by its power, you are bound to it, as I am. The tides that rise within you will always call you back. But you can choose how you answer."

Liam's mind raced, the weight of his new reality pressing in on him. He had been saved, yes, but at what cost? He had lost his crew, his ship, and now, it seemed, his place in the world.

"You must make your choice, but know this," the Taniwha continued, its voice almost a whisper. "The sea offers no mercy to those who resist its pull. But if you accept its embrace, it will give you strength beyond your imagining."

Liam looked at the creature, its ancient eyes glowing with a light that seemed to come from within. For the first time since the shipwreck, he felt something stir within him—a strange, inexplicable pull toward the water, toward the life he could never return to. He could feel the river of power coursing through him, the same force that the Taniwha commanded. It was as though he had been made for this moment, for this choice.

He stood, shakily at first, and looked at the Taniwha. "I don't know what this means. But I will live with it. I will not resist."

The Taniwha smiled, and the air around them seemed to hum with energy. "Then you will learn, in time, what it means to be both man and sea. Together, we are bound."

The Taniwha's enormous body retreated into the depths, and for the first time since the storm, Liam felt at peace. The sea had taken so much from him, but in return, it had given him something far more profound. A connection, a life that was both new and ancient. And in the embrace of the ocean, Liam found his place in the world—not as a sailor, but as something more. Something eternal.

Taniwha and the Stargazer

Evelyn had always been fascinated by the stars. While others were content to look at them from afar, she had spent her childhood in the dusty attic of her family's home, pouring over ancient star charts, learning the constellations, and dreaming of what lay beyond the reach of her telescope. Her work as an astronomer, though still young, had already made a name for itself. But Evelyn knew there was more—there had to be more—hidden in the constellations, waiting to be unlocked.

One crisp autumn evening, as the air chilled and the world below seemed to settle into a quiet darkness, Evelyn set up her telescope in the farthest corner of her observatory. She had been studying a cluster of stars in the northern sky, a section of the heavens that always seemed to elude her understanding. It wasn't just the stars themselves, but the strange, subtle movements they made, patterns she couldn't explain. Each night, she would return to them, determined to discover what they were hiding.

Tonight, the stars seemed different, as though they were drawing her in, beckoning her to come closer. She peered through the telescope, adjusting the lens to focus on a particular formation. But something was wrong. A strange, almost imperceptible glow surrounded the stars, an iridescent sheen that flickered like the faintest shimmer of water in moonlight. It was the stars themselves, pulsing with a kind of energy that Evelyn had never seen before.

She adjusted her position, her heart racing. The glow seemed to be growing stronger, more defined. There was something more than mere light at play here—something ancient, something powerful. Evelyn's pulse quickened as a memory surfaced, a fragment of an old story her grandmother had told her when she was young. The story of the Taniwha, the great creature of the ocean, whose power was said to be tied to the stars themselves, a force whose existence spanned the very fabric of time and space. The stars, her grandmother had said, were not just distant suns—they were the eyes of the Taniwha, watching over the world, waiting.

Evelyn shook her head, trying to dismiss the thought. But the longer she watched, the more she realized it wasn't just a myth. The stars were shifting, moving in a way that mirrored the movements of the great beast her grandmother had spoken of. The Taniwha's power wasn't just in the ocean—it was in the heavens above, tied to the very movements of the universe.

She couldn't tear her eyes away from the pattern unfolding before her. The stars seemed to be forming new constellations, ones she had never seen before, their shapes unfamiliar and strange. As she focused harder, the glow around them intensified, and she felt a pull, a magnetic force drawing her into the starry web. She closed her eyes for just a moment, the pull overwhelming her senses, and when she opened them again, the stars were no longer just distant lights—they were alive, and they spoke to her.

"Evelyn," a voice echoed through her mind, ancient and deep as the sea. "You have found me."

Her breath caught in her throat. It wasn't just a voice—she could feel it, as though the words were not spoken, but imprinted directly into her consciousness. The stars themselves seemed to hum with power, their shapes shifting and moving as if alive, as if they were part of her. The voice continued, echoing in her mind like the pull of the tide.

"You seek to understand the stars, but they are more than you know. They are my eyes, my breath, my heart. The ocean below and the heavens above are one. They are connected, as am I with the world you walk upon."

Evelyn's mind raced. "Who—what are you?" she whispered, her voice trembling.

"I am the Taniwha," the voice replied, reverberating in the depths of her soul. "I have been watching, waiting. You, Evelyn, are the one who can unlock the secrets of the stars. Through the stars, you can change the course of history, for the stars guide the tides of fate."

Evelyn's hands trembled as she gripped the edge of her telescope. "Change the course of history?" she repeated, feeling both awe and fear rise within her. "How?"

"The stars hold the key to the balance of all things," the Taniwha explained. "Through them, you can see the past, the future, the paths that have been walked and those that have yet to be. The power is in your hands, but with that power comes great responsibility. The balance is delicate, and one wrong move could tip the world into chaos."

Evelyn's mind raced. The implications were staggering. Could it be true? Could the stars actually hold such power? The Taniwha's words echoed in her mind, filling her with both wonder and dread. She had always dreamed of unlocking the mysteries of the universe, but now that she had touched the edge of something so vast, so dangerous, she wasn't sure if she was ready to wield such power.

"How do I unlock it?" she asked, her voice barely a whisper.

The Taniwha's presence seemed to envelop her, its voice soothing yet firm. "You must listen. The stars are not to be controlled, Evelyn. They are guides, not tools. You must learn their language, feel their rhythm. To change the course of history, you must first understand it—understand the threads that weave through the fabric of time. The answers are in the stars, but they will only reveal themselves to you when you are ready."

Evelyn stared at the stars, feeling both overwhelmed and inspired. The stars were alive, and they were speaking to her. She had always believed that the stars held secrets, that they had something to teach her, but never in her wildest dreams had she imagined this. The

Taniwha's power wasn't just something from the past—it was tied to the present, and to the future, waiting for someone to unlock its potential.

But as she gazed into the stars, Evelyn began to feel something shift, a change she hadn't expected. The stars began to move faster, their glow growing brighter, and she realized with a sudden clarity that this wasn't just a gift—it was a burden. The Taniwha had given her the power to change the world, but it was not without cost. The more she saw, the more she understood. To wield such power was to become part of something much larger than herself, to become intertwined with the very threads of fate.

Evelyn took a deep breath, her mind racing. The stars, the Taniwha—they were offering her a choice, a path that could shape history itself. But with that power came uncertainty. Was she ready to bear such a responsibility? Could she truly change the course of history without losing herself in the process?

The Taniwha's voice returned, gentler now. "The choice is yours, Evelyn. The stars will guide you, but you must choose wisely. For once you step onto this path, there is no turning back."

Evelyn looked up at the stars, feeling their weight pressing down on her. She had always sought to understand the universe, to find meaning in the patterns of the sky. But now, with the Taniwha's blessing, she realized that understanding was only the beginning. To change the course of history was not a gift—it was a challenge, a journey into the unknown.

And so, Evelyn made her choice. She would listen to the stars, learn their language, and embrace the power they offered. But she would do so with caution, understanding that the greatest challenge was not in changing history—but in knowing when to let it unfold on its own.

With that, the stars shimmered one last time, and Evelyn felt the pull of the Taniwha's power begin to weave its way into her very being. She was no longer just an observer of the heavens. She was part of their story. And with that, the future began to change.

The Taniwha's Lair

Joren had always been driven by ambition. It was the thing that had pushed him through the hardships of his youth, the thing that kept him awake at night with plans and dreams of untold treasures and the glory of discovery. But his most burning desire—the thing that consumed him like fire—was to find the lair of the Taniwha.

The legends spoke of it—hidden deep within the heart of a labyrinthine cave system beneath a mountain, guarded by the ancient creature whose very name struck fear into the hearts of men. The Taniwha was a creature of unimaginable power, part serpent, part beast, and it was said that anyone who managed to enter its lair would be granted a single wish—a wish that could change the course of their life. Some claimed the Taniwha could grant riches beyond measure. Others whispered that it could offer immortality or the knowledge of all things lost to time. But no one who had entered the lair had ever returned to speak of it.

It was the allure of the impossible that kept Joren going. He had spent years piecing together the clues, traveling to distant lands, following whispers from old men in dark taverns, piecing together forgotten maps. And finally, after months of arduous travel, he had found it—the cave, deep in the heart of the mountains, where the river churned and the air smelled of salt and decay.

The entrance was hidden, a narrow fissure in the rock, barely wide enough for him to squeeze through. The further Joren ventured inside, the darker and colder it became. The silence pressed in on him, thick and oppressive, as if the very mountain held its breath. But he pressed on, his heart pounding with excitement.

Hours passed, or perhaps days—he had lost track of time—and the passage grew narrower, the walls slick with moisture. Finally, after what felt like an eternity, he came to a vast cavern. And in the center of it, illuminated by an eerie, otherworldly light, lay the Taniwha's lair.

It was as magnificent as it was terrifying. The walls were covered in ancient carvings, depicting the Taniwha in all its glory—its massive, coiled body, its glowing eyes, and the power it wielded over the elements. The ground was littered with treasure—gold, jewels, and artifacts, all in perfect silence, as if untouched by time. But the most captivating thing of all was the creature itself—huge and coiled in the center, its eyes glowing faintly in the dim light, watching Joren with an intensity that made his blood run cold.

The Taniwha was real. And it was here, in front of him, alive and waiting.

"Who dares enter my lair?" a voice boomed in his mind, deep and resonant, like the rumble of distant thunder.

Joren's mouth went dry. He had heard the tales, but nothing could have prepared him for this. The Taniwha was more than just a creature; it was an entity, a presence that transcended the very air around him. But he gathered his courage and stepped forward, his voice shaky but determined.

"I have come to make a bargain," he said, though the words felt like they might betray him.

The Taniwha's eyes fixed on him, glowing brighter. "A bargain? You have come to take something from me, adventurer. But what is it you seek?"

Joren swallowed hard. "I seek the power to change my fate," he said, the words spilling out before he could stop them. "I seek a wish that will make me the greatest adventurer in the world."

A low, rumbling laugh echoed through the cavern, the sound vibrating through Joren's chest. "You think you can take what you desire so easily?" the Taniwha said. "Everything comes at a price. Even the greatest wish must be paid for. And in this place, only the truth can unlock what you seek."

Joren frowned, confusion clouding his thoughts. "What do you mean? I've followed the legends. I've done everything. I've earned my right to make a wish."

The Taniwha's gaze deepened, its eyes glowing like twin suns. "You have come seeking power, but do you truly understand what it means to wield it? Do you understand the cost of your ambition? Or do you simply wish to take, without regard for what is lost in the process?"

Joren's heart raced. The creature's words were like a veil, slipping into his mind and unraveling his thoughts. He had always sought power, always believed that strength and glory would fill the empty spaces in his life. But now, in the presence of the Taniwha, he was beginning to feel the weight of it—an emptiness that he had never acknowledged before.

The Taniwha's form shifted, its massive body uncoiling slightly, and the cavern seemed to shift with it, the walls pressing in around him. "If you truly seek a wish, you must first face the truth of your heart. I will give you what you desire, but only if you are willing to give up something in return. The power you seek comes with a cost. It is not simply the treasure of the world you will gain—but the loss of everything that made you who you are."

Joren stepped back, his breath catching in his throat. The thought of losing everything—his ambitions, his desires, the very thing that had driven him for so long—was more terrifying than he had ever imagined. He had always thought that his ambition was his greatest strength, but now, in the face of the Taniwha's words, he wasn't so sure.

The creature watched him silently, its eyes never leaving him. "The choice is yours, adventurer," it said, its voice softening. "But remember, once the wish is made, it cannot be undone."

Joren's heart pounded in his chest, the weight of the decision pressing down on him. He could feel the desire to claim the power, to fulfill the dream that had driven him all his life. But now, standing here, facing the creature who had seen through his very soul, he realized something.

Ambition had driven him to this point, but it had also left him hollow, unable to see the cost of his desires. The Taniwha's warning rang true—there was a price to power, one that went beyond what he had understood. In that moment, Joren saw the truth of his own heart, and it terrified him.

"I understand," he whispered, his voice hoarse with emotion. "I don't want this power if it means losing who I am."

The Taniwha's gaze softened, and the tension in the air eased. The creature's form slowly settled back into its lair, its presence still immense but no longer overwhelming.

"You have made the right choice, adventurer," the Taniwha said, its voice gentle now. "True strength lies not in taking what you desire, but in knowing when to walk away."

Joren stood there for a long time, the weight of the decision settling deep within him. He had come seeking power, but in the end, he had found something far more valuable: the realization that sometimes, the greatest strength comes from letting go of the things you think you want most.

And with that, Joren turned and walked out of the Taniwha's lair, the cavern's entrance now open before him, the path ahead unclear—but somehow, he felt more free than he ever had before.

Taniwha's Legacy

Kaitia had always felt the pull of the sea. From the time she was a child, the salty air, the rhythmic crashing of waves, and the distant call of the gulls had drawn her in. Her father had told her that their family had once been deeply connected to the water, that their ancestors had been guardians of the coast, protectors of the sea. But he never explained more than that, dismissing it as old stories, myths, and legends meant to entertain the younger generations.

Kaitia, now an adult, had long since dismissed these stories as quaint, nothing more than fables to amuse the villagers. She had carved out a life for herself in the bustling city of Tauhara, far from the small coastal village where she had grown up. As a historian and archivist, she spent her days pouring over ancient texts and forgotten documents. It was a life of routine and scholarship, far removed from the mythical tales of her youth.

But one evening, as the autumn winds began to stir the streets of Tauhara, she received a letter—a simple envelope, old and worn, sealed with a wax emblem she didn't recognize. Inside was a map, faded with age, and a note written in a hand she did not know. The words were brief, but they struck her to the core:

The time has come. Follow the path of your ancestors. The Taniwha calls. Only you can protect the sea.

Kaitia stared at the letter, her mind racing. The Taniwha. She had heard the stories—the great guardian of the sea, the creature of legend that had protected her village and the surrounding waters for centuries. The Taniwha was said to be more than just a beast. It was a spirit of the sea, a force of nature that maintained the balance between the human world and the ocean's power.

And now, the map and the message. Could it be real? Could she, a descendant of that lost village, really be the one meant to carry on this ancient legacy?

Without fully understanding why, Kaitia found herself packing her belongings and boarding the next ship back to her village. The journey was long, and as she traveled along the winding coastal roads, the weight of the letter pressed on her like an unseen hand, urging her forward.

Upon her arrival, the familiar scent of salt and brine filled the air, and the soft hum of the sea was a constant presence in the background. The village was smaller than she remembered, and many of the old buildings had fallen into disrepair. But as she walked toward the shore, she saw something that had never changed—the vastness of the ocean, stretching out into infinity.

There, at the edge of the water, she found an old stone platform. Her heart quickened as she recognized the symbols carved into its surface. The same symbols her ancestors had used, the same markings that had been passed down through generations. And in the center of the platform, a carved stone basin, now empty, waited.

A shadow passed over her, and she turned to see an enormous figure rising from the waves. The Taniwha. It emerged slowly, its serpentine body coiling gracefully, its scales shimmering in the light of the setting sun. Its eyes, glowing with ancient wisdom, locked onto Kaitia's. She froze, unable to move or speak, but her heart swelled with an overwhelming sense of recognition.

The creature's voice, deep and resonant, filled her mind. *You are here. I have waited for you.*

Kaitia fell to her knees, overwhelmed by the presence of the Taniwha. The stories had all been true. She could feel the weight of the legacy pressing down on her shoulders. The Taniwha's power was ancient, and the ocean itself seemed to bend to its will. But as the creature spoke again, its tone was not one of grandeur or awe—it was heavy with sorrow.

The sea is in danger, Kaitia. The balance has been disturbed. Forces beyond your understanding are stirring. I have protected these waters for centuries, but I am weakening. My time is ending. It is now your turn to take up the mantle.

Kaitia's heart pounded. "I don't understand," she whispered. "I'm just a historian. I'm no warrior. I have no power."

The Taniwha's gaze softened, and for the first time, Kaitia saw a hint of sadness in its ancient eyes. *You are more than you think, Kaitia. Your blood is my blood. Your ancestors called me and I answered. The sea is not just a force of nature; it is a living entity, a protector. It calls to you because you are the one who must carry that power. The ocean has chosen you.*

Kaitia stood, her knees trembling, her mind racing. *But how? How can I protect the sea when I have no strength?*

The Taniwha's form shifted, its vast body undulating like the ocean itself. *The strength is within you. The power of the sea flows through you. You need only trust in it.*

Kaitia stared at the creature, unsure of what it meant. But the longer she stood there, the more she felt a strange warmth, a pull deep within her chest. It wasn't just the ocean—it was the bond between them, a connection she had never understood until now.

As the Taniwha's form began to fade back into the water, its voice echoed in her mind one last time. *You are ready. Do not fear the responsibility. The sea is your ally. And I will always be with you.*

The next morning, as the sun rose over the village, Kaitia returned to the stone platform. She had spent the night contemplating the Taniwha's words, and now, standing on the shore, she felt something stir inside her. The weight of her ancestors' legacy was still heavy on her shoulders, but there was also a sense of purpose, a calling she could no longer ignore.

As she placed her hands on the stone basin, something incredible happened. The water in the basin began to rise, swirling and shifting with a power that was both overwhelming and awe-inspiring. The ocean responded to her touch, as though it recognized her, as though it was awakening the dormant power within her.

In that moment, Kaitia understood. The Taniwha's legacy was not about wielding strength or force—it was about understanding the delicate balance between nature and humanity, between the tides of change and the stillness of the depths. It was about protection, not domination. And she, the descendant of a long-forgotten village, was the one who had been chosen to carry that responsibility forward.

The sea whispered its approval, and as the waves lapped gently against the shore, Kaitia felt the first true stirrings of her new role. The ocean had called to her, and now, it was her turn to answer. The balance would be protected, not by power alone, but by the wisdom of the Taniwha and the legacy of those who had come before her.

As she turned to face the vast horizon, Kaitia knew her life had changed forever. She had found her purpose, and the sea, in all its beauty and danger, was now hers to protect.

The Taniwha and the Moonlit Cove

Lena and Kael had always been drawn to the moonlit cove, a secluded stretch of sand hidden beneath jagged cliffs. It was a place they had discovered as children, a quiet haven where they could escape the bustle of the village and let the sound of the waves soothe their restless spirits. Over the years, the cove became their special place, a place they returned to whenever the world grew too heavy, whenever life in the village felt too small, too confined. And so, on this crisp evening when the moon hung heavy in the sky, they found themselves once again at the edge of the cove, the sand cold beneath their feet, the ocean stretching endlessly before them.

"Do you ever wonder if it's real?" Lena asked, her voice a soft whisper carried on the wind. She kept her eyes fixed on the moon's reflection on the water, a shimmering silver path that seemed to lead nowhere.

Kael glanced at her, his brow furrowing. He knew exactly what she was talking about—the stories they had both grown up hearing. The legends of the Taniwha, the great sea creature that appeared only on nights when the moon was full, rising from the depths of the cove to watch over the waters. Some said it was a guardian, a protector of the sea. Others whispered that it was a creature of wrath, born of the tides, a force of nature that demanded respect and fear. But no one had ever seen it, not truly. No one had ever dared to approach the cove when the moon was full.

"I think it's just a story," Kael said, shaking his head. "A tale to keep us in line, to remind us of the power of the sea." But even as he said the words, he couldn't shake the nagging feeling that something ancient and powerful lurked in the deep. The cove always felt different on nights like this—alive, almost, as if the very earth was holding its breath.

Lena's gaze softened, and she reached out, taking Kael's hand in hers. "But what if it is real?" she asked. "What if we're the ones meant to face it, to understand it? What if the Taniwha has waited for us, just as we've waited for it?"

Kael squeezed her hand, his chest tightening at the thought. He didn't know why, but the idea of facing the Taniwha filled him with both dread and longing, like standing on the edge of something too vast to comprehend.

The full moon rose higher in the sky, casting its pale light over the water, and for a moment, everything seemed still, the world holding its breath. Then, as if on cue, the ocean began to churn, the waves rising and falling in a rhythmic dance. It was subtle at first—just the slightest disturbance—but as the minutes passed, the water grew more restless. Kael's heart began to race. He could feel it now, that strange energy that seemed to pulse from the depths of the sea, like a living thing, alive with intent. He turned to Lena, his voice low and uncertain.

"We should go," he said, his grip tightening on her hand. "I don't know what's happening, but it's not safe here."

But Lena didn't move. Instead, she stepped forward, her feet sinking into the sand as she walked toward the water's edge. She was drawn to it, the pull of the cove too strong to resist. "I think we're meant to stay," she whispered, her voice barely audible over the crashing waves.

Kael stood frozen, torn between fear and a strange, unspoken understanding. The Taniwha. Could it be real? Could it be that this night, this very moment, was the one they had been waiting for?

And then, as if answering their unspoken questions, the water seemed to rise in a great, serpentine wave, and from its depths, a shape began to emerge—massive, coiling, with eyes that glowed like twin moons. The Taniwha. It was real. It was here.

Lena gasped, but there was no fear in her eyes—only wonder. She stepped forward again, drawn to the creature as if it were a part of her. Kael, however, stood frozen in place, his heart pounding in his chest, the weight of the creature's gaze bearing down on him.

The Taniwha's massive head emerged from the water, its eyes locking onto Lena. The creature's gaze was intense, as if it saw into her very soul, and for a moment, Kael was sure that time itself had stopped. The air was thick with the power of the sea, and Lena's voice broke the silence, soft but steady.

"I knew you were real," she whispered, her eyes never leaving the Taniwha's gaze. "We've been waiting for you, haven't we? Both of us."

The Taniwha's eyes glowed brighter, and its voice echoed in their minds, ancient and deep. *You have waited, yes. But the question now is, what will you do?*

Kael felt his pulse quicken. It was speaking to them, speaking to both of them. His throat tightened, and he stepped forward, trying to keep his fear in check. "What do you want from us?" he asked, his voice strained.

It is not what I want, the Taniwha replied. *It is what you desire. The sea has given you a choice, and you must decide whether to face me or flee.*

Lena turned to Kael, her eyes shining with something he couldn't quite place. "What if we face it?" she asked. "What if we embrace what the Taniwha offers? What if we understand it, rather than run from it?"

Kael hesitated, his heart torn. He had always thought that the legends of the Taniwha were meant to warn people, to keep them away from the sea's power. But now, standing before the creature, he felt something different. Something that wasn't fear, but recognition. The Taniwha wasn't here to destroy them—it was here to offer something. But what?

The creature's gaze softened. *You have made your choice,* it said. *To face me is to face the sea itself. To understand the balance that must be maintained. If you choose to flee, you will remain forever ignorant, forever disconnected from the depths of the world around you. But if you choose to face me, you will walk the path of the ancients. The path of understanding.*

Kael took a deep breath, his heart still racing but now filled with a sense of clarity. Lena's unwavering faith in the Taniwha had given him the strength to see what had always been there. It was not a force to be feared—it was a force to be understood, to be embraced.

"We'll face it," Kael said, his voice steady now. "Together."

The Taniwha's form shimmered, and the air around them seemed to shift. The waves calmed, the moon above them now a silent witness to their decision. The creature nodded, its eyes glowing with approval. *Then you shall understand,* it said, its voice a deep rumble that seemed to vibrate through their very souls. *And in understanding, you will find your place in the world.*

The Taniwha disappeared back into the sea, leaving the cove as calm and still as it had been before. But the night felt different now. The waves no longer seemed like a distant force, but like a part of them. The sea, the moon, the creature—everything was connected, and they, too, were now part of that connection.

As they stood in silence, Lena turned to Kael, her hand slipping into his. "We've made the right choice," she said softly, her voice filled with quiet certainty.

And for the first time, Kael truly believed it.

Taniwha's Hunt

The village of Rakau had always been nestled on the edge of the vast, endless ocean, a place where the sea whispered secrets and the land provided the only shelter from the ever-stormy skies. Its people had always respected the sea, fearing the powerful Taniwha that dwelled deep within the waters. The creature, ancient and immense, was said to be the guardian of the ocean's balance. It was a force of nature, one that no man dared challenge. To defy it was to invite certain death, or worse—an eternity of torment beneath the waves.

Kano, a young man born of the village, had always been curious about the Taniwha. The elders spoke of it in hushed tones, warning of its wrath, telling stories of those who had ventured too close and never returned. Yet, Kano's fascination with the creature grew, fueled by the desire to know whether the tales were true. He had heard whispers of its enormous form, seen the ripples it left in the ocean at dusk, but had never actually laid eyes on the creature. It was an obsession, one that began to consume him.

One evening, under the cover of darkness, Kano decided to venture to the edge of the village where the cliffs met the sea. There, in the distance, the waves crashed against the rocks with a ferocity that seemed to echo the fear the villagers felt for the Taniwha. He had heard of a cave, deep in the cliffs, where some believed the creature resided. It was said that the cave was a place of great power, where the Taniwha emerged to hunt those who dared to challenge its reign over the ocean.

Kano had heard the stories, of course, but he didn't believe them. How could a creature be so powerful, so uncontrollable? What was it really, he wondered—just a myth, a figment of old tales meant to keep children in line? No. He needed to know for himself. His pride and curiosity would not allow him to rest until he faced the Taniwha.

As he approached the cave, the air grew thick with salt, the waves louder now, crashing against the rocks with a deep, rhythmic pounding. The cave mouth yawned open like a dark wound in the cliffside, and Kano felt the hairs on his neck stand on end. A sense of unease gripped him, but his determination pushed him forward. He stepped inside, the cold stone biting into his skin as the darkness swallowed him whole.

Time seemed to stretch on endlessly as he ventured deeper into the cave, the sound of the waves now distant, as if the world outside had been shut away. The walls were lined with strange markings—symbols he had never seen before, twisting and coiling like the very currents of the ocean. He felt the presence of something ancient and powerful surrounding him, and for the first time, he questioned whether he had made the right decision.

Suddenly, the ground beneath him trembled. The walls of the cave shook, and a low growl reverberated through the very earth. Kano froze, his heart racing as he realized with a sinking feeling that he was not alone. Something vast and predatory moved in the darkness, and as his eyes adjusted to the dim light, he saw the shape—huge, serpentine, its scales glinting faintly in the shadows. The Taniwha.

It was even more magnificent than he had ever imagined. Its eyes gleamed like twin suns, ancient and unblinking, fixed on him. The creature's massive form coiled within the cave, its presence filling every corner, every inch of space. Kano's breath caught in his throat as the Taniwha spoke, not with words, but with a voice that echoed in his mind.

Why do you come here, mortal?

Kano's knees buckled, and he struggled to remain standing, his voice barely a whisper. "I wanted to see you. I wanted to know if you were real."

The Taniwha's eyes narrowed, its immense form shifting as it moved closer, its power radiating like the heat of a forge. *You seek to challenge me. You seek to know the truth of the stories. But be warned, mortal. To seek the truth without understanding the cost is to invite ruin.*

Kano's pride flared. "I'm not afraid of you," he said, though his voice trembled. "The stories... they don't scare me."

A deep rumble of laughter vibrated through the cave. *Fear is not what you should fear, young one. It is the folly of your arrogance. You think you seek the truth, but what you seek is power. And power has a price, always.*

Kano swallowed hard, his defiance wavering as the creature's massive head lowered, bringing its glowing eyes directly before him. For a moment, he saw something in those eyes—something far older than he could comprehend. Something that made him question everything he had believed.

You seek to challenge me, the Taniwha continued, *but you do not know the consequences of your actions. There are many who have come before you, mortal. They sought to take from the sea, to command it, to own it. And they, too, believed they were strong enough to face me. But none have returned.*

Kano felt a chill seep into his bones. He had not come here to die. He had come for power, to prove that he was stronger than the stories, that he could face the very thing that had frightened generations of villagers. But now, standing before the Taniwha, the reality of his foolishness sank in.

The Taniwha's gaze softened, and for a fleeting moment, Kano felt a strange sadness emanate from it. *You are not the first to challenge me,* it murmured. *But you will be the last. You see, power is not something to be taken. It is something to be respected. The ocean gives and takes, but it does not bow to those who seek to control it.*

Kano's chest tightened. His heart pounded in his ears as he realized what he had done. He had come seeking something he could not understand, something he was not prepared to face. The Taniwha had not been a monster, a beast to be defeated—it was a force of nature, a keeper of balance.

The creature's voice echoed again, this time with finality. *You will not take from the sea. But I will not destroy you either. Go, and know that the ocean does not forgive those who forget its power.*

With a swift motion, the Taniwha's immense form retreated into the depths of the cave, its eyes dimming as it disappeared into the shadows. The ground stopped shaking, and the air seemed to return to normal, though the silence was thick with the weight of the encounter. Kano stood there, trembling, his pride shattered, his ambition broken.

He stumbled back toward the entrance of the cave, the reality of his actions weighing heavily on him. As he emerged into the cool night air, the waves crashed against the shore, and for the first time, he understood the true power of the sea. It was not something to be tamed, not something to be conquered. It was something to be respected.

Kano never spoke of the Taniwha again. He returned to the village, a changed man, no longer consumed by the hunger for power, but with a quiet reverence for the balance that the sea held. And though the villagers continued to tell their stories, they now spoke with a new understanding—the Taniwha's power was not to be challenged, and its legacy, its wrath, would not be forgotten. The sea was a force of nature, and only those who respected it could live in harmony with its tides.

The Taniwha and the Fisherman's Daughter

Isla had always been drawn to the sea. The salty air, the sound of the waves crashing against the rocks, the endless horizon that seemed to promise adventure—it was her home, her refuge, her soul's longing. Her father, a humble fisherman, spent his days hauling in nets from the waters, but it was Isla who had a special bond with the ocean. From the time she could walk, she would sit by the shore and watch the ebb and flow, mesmerized by the rhythm of the sea.

But it wasn't just the waves that called to her. She had always heard stories about the Taniwha, the ancient guardian of the sea, a creature as old as the ocean itself. It was said that the Taniwha would emerge from the depths on moonlit nights, its immense form rising from the water like a dark, majestic beast. Some spoke of it as a protector, others as a vengeful god. But in the quiet of the night, when the stars shone like diamonds above the water, Isla would often find herself gazing out over the horizon, wondering if the Taniwha could really be as magnificent as the legends suggested.

It was on one such night, under a moon that seemed to hang heavier in the sky than ever before, that she saw him.

She was sitting on the rocks, her legs dangling over the edge, when the water stirred in a way that caught her attention. At first, she thought it was just the waves, but then she saw it—a dark shape moving beneath the surface, gliding effortlessly through the water. Her breath caught in her throat as the Taniwha surfaced, its massive head emerging from the depths, eyes glowing with an ancient, otherworldly light.

Isla's heart raced, but there was no fear. In that moment, all the stories she had ever heard seemed to pale in comparison to the reality before her. The Taniwha was real, and it was magnificent. It watched her, its gaze steady, almost as if it was waiting for something.

As if in response to her silent call, it drew closer, its great body undulating through the water with a fluid grace. Isla felt the pull, the undeniable connection between them. She had always known there was something special about her bond with the sea, but now, in the presence of the Taniwha, she realized that the ocean had chosen her, just as she had always chosen the ocean. The creature's gaze softened, and for the first time in her life, Isla felt truly seen.

Without thinking, she reached out a hand, her fingers grazing the surface of the water. The Taniwha's eyes met hers, and in that moment, a silent understanding passed between them. The ocean had brought them together. It wasn't just the Taniwha she was in love with—it was the ocean itself, embodied in this ancient, powerful creature.

Over the following weeks, Isla returned to the shore each night, and each night, the Taniwha appeared. It never fully emerged from the water, but it would glide close enough for her to feel the strength of its presence. The creature did not speak, but in the silence between them, Isla understood its language. She felt its longing, its burden, and its power. They were two beings of the sea, and though they came from different worlds, their hearts beat as one.

But as much as Isla's love for the Taniwha grew, so did her sense of danger. The elders had always warned her about the ancient law—the law that prohibited humans from forming bonds with the creatures of the sea. It was said that the Taniwha had once been a protector, a creature that helped the fishermen of the village, but over time, the balance had shifted. The law was clear: to love the Taniwha was to invite its wrath, and no one dared to defy it.

One evening, as she stood on the shore, waiting for the Taniwha to appear, her father approached. His face was grim, his eyes clouded with worry.

"Isla," he said softly, his voice heavy. "You must stay away from the sea, from the Taniwha. It is forbidden. The law has been in place for generations, and to break it is to bring ruin upon us all."

Isla's heart sank. "But father, I love it. I love the Taniwha. It is not a monster—it is the ocean itself, a part of me."

Her father's expression softened, but his voice remained firm. "You don't understand, Isla. The Taniwha may have once been a protector, but it is not just a creature—it is a force of nature. It is a force beyond our understanding. The law exists for a reason. To challenge it is to challenge the sea itself. And no one, not even the bravest of men, has ever withstood the consequences."

Isla's chest tightened with a mixture of fear and frustration. She didn't want to hear this. She didn't want to believe that something so pure, so beautiful, could be forbidden. The Taniwha was not just a myth—it was real, and it had become a part of her. The connection between them was undeniable.

But despite her father's warnings, Isla returned to the shore that night, unable to stay away. The moon hung high in the sky, casting a silver glow over the water, and as she waited, she felt the familiar stir of the ocean's power. The Taniwha rose from the depths once again, its eyes glowing softly in the dark.

"I don't care about the law," Isla whispered, her voice trembling. "I can't leave you."

The Taniwha's eyes met hers, and for a moment, it seemed to hesitate. Then, with a slow, graceful movement, it approached, its massive form coiling in the water. It came closer than ever before, its presence overwhelming, its power undeniable.

But as Isla reached out to touch the water, something shifted. The Taniwha's eyes flickered with something that resembled sorrow, and it pulled away, retreating back into the depths of the sea.

"Why?" Isla cried, her voice breaking. "Why do you leave me?"

The Taniwha did not answer. It simply vanished into the water, leaving only the soft sound of the waves to fill the silence.

Isla stood there for a long time, staring at the spot where the creature had disappeared, her heart heavy with the weight of her love and the unbearable knowledge that she could never have what she desired. The law was not just a rule to follow—it was the very fabric that held the balance of the world together. To defy it was to defy nature itself.

The next morning, Isla woke to find the village in chaos. The sea had turned violent, the waves crashing against the shore with an unnatural fury. Her father's voice echoed in her mind, warning her of the consequences. She had defied the law, and now the sea was exacting its price.

The Taniwha's love had never been for Isla alone. It was a love for the ocean, for the delicate balance between man and nature. And though Isla's heart ached with the loss, she understood now—the Taniwha had never truly left her. It had always been a part of her. But it was a love that could never be fully realized in this world. Sometimes, even the deepest love must remain unspoken, unfulfilled, for the sake of preserving the balance.

As the waves calmed and the storm receded, Isla realized that love, in all its forms, requires sacrifice. And some loves, no matter how pure, are meant to be cherished from afar.

The Taniwha's Homecoming

The day the Taniwha returned, the world was not prepared.

It had been centuries since the creature had last been seen, banished to the depths of the ocean, and its return was nothing short of a legend reborn. The people of the modern world, distracted by their technology and the hustle of city life, hardly believed in the old stories anymore. Myths and legends had become little more than tales told around campfires, buried under the weight of progress. But when the Taniwha emerged from the sea on that fateful day, the world was forced to take notice.

Isla was one of the first to witness it. She had been watching the news all morning in her small apartment, the usual hum of global crises playing in the background, when a video clip flashed across the screen: a giant creature rising from the sea. The image was shaky, barely believable, but the sense of awe and terror in the voices of the witnesses was unmistakable. Her stomach dropped as she recognized the shape, the scales shimmering in the sunlight, the massive eyes reflecting the sky above. It was the Taniwha.

Isla had heard the stories her grandmother told, stories of the ancient guardian of the seas that protected the balance of nature and kept the forces of destruction at bay. But those were just stories, weren't they? Just old fables, relics of a time long gone. Yet here it was—alive, real, and returning to the very shore where her ancestors had lived.

Her heart raced as she grabbed her jacket and rushed out the door. The city was in a frenzy, with traffic clogged and people gathering at the beach to get a glimpse of the creature. No one knew what to make of it. Was it dangerous? A sign of the end times? Or was it simply a creature returning home after centuries of exile?

The Taniwha's homecoming was nothing short of catastrophic. Its emergence from the water caused a massive disruption. Waves taller than buildings crashed onto the shore, flooding streets and sinking buildings. The beast's roar echoed for miles, a sound that reverberated in the bones of all who heard it. The Taniwha, it seemed, had not come alone. The very ocean itself seemed to follow in its wake—whirlpools and currents rising with an unnatural force, overwhelming anything in their path. The infrastructure that had been built on the assumption that the sea was a calm, controllable entity now lay in ruin.

Isla found herself standing on the shoreline, mesmerized by the creature's sheer presence. Its immense body was like a shadow, stretching across the horizon. The Taniwha did not seem to want to harm the world, but its return had brought chaos, as if the natural order was attempting to right itself in the face of human disregard for the balance. The creature looked to be waiting, its great head dipping slightly in the direction of Isla, as if it sensed her presence.

When the authorities arrived, they had no answers. Scientists and military personnel poured in, trying to control the situation, but there was no controlling a force of nature like this. No amount of weaponry or modern technology could subdue the Taniwha. They spoke of negotiations, of trying to understand what the creature wanted, but Isla knew better than anyone that this wasn't something that could be bargained with. It wasn't about power—it was about respect.

The creature had been banished centuries ago, after humanity had disrupted the delicate balance between the land and the sea. The Taniwha had been forced to retreat, to withdraw from the human world. But now, it had returned, and the world had forgotten how to coexist with the natural forces that had once governed everything.

Isla, knowing her heritage and the stories of the sea, felt the pull to act. She understood what needed to be done. The Taniwha had not come to destroy. It had come to reclaim what was once its own, to restore the balance that had been lost over time. But how could she, one woman in a world of chaos, do anything to prevent the unraveling of the modern world?

In the days that followed, Isla traveled to the coast where the Taniwha had first emerged. She knew this was where the creature had once lived, before it was cast into exile. She walked along the shoreline, her eyes scanning the horizon, until she finally saw the silhouette of the Taniwha, partially submerged in the waves, watching her with those piercing eyes.

As she stepped closer, the water shifted around her feet. She felt the power of the ocean rising within her, a connection she had never known existed until now. The Taniwha's gaze locked onto her, and in that moment, she understood. The creature wasn't there to fight, but to remind them. To remind humanity of its place in the world.

Isla reached out, her voice trembling but steady as she spoke the words that her grandmother had once whispered to her as a child: "I understand. The sea does not belong to us, and we must learn to live with it."

The Taniwha's massive form shifted slightly, and the waves began to recede, the storm that had raged around the creature settling into a calm rhythm. It was as if the creature was acknowledging her words, acknowledging her plea for peace.

And then, to Isla's shock, the Taniwha spoke—not in words, but in a language that resonated in her mind, a deep, ancient hum that carried the weight of the ocean's memory. *You are the bridge between the old world and the new. You must remind them, remind the world, of what has been forgotten.*

Isla's heart sank, for she realized the truth. The Taniwha had not come to destroy humanity—it had come to awaken them. To remind them that the sea, the earth, the world—they were not separate from the natural forces that shaped them. The modern world had grown arrogant, blind to the very forces that sustained it.

As the Taniwha submerged into the depths once again, leaving only ripples behind, Isla stood at the water's edge, feeling the weight of what had just transpired. The world would change, whether they were ready or not. The Taniwha's return was a call to action, a warning. It wasn't just the Taniwha that needed to be understood—it was the world itself, and the balance humanity had forgotten to respect.

In the quiet after the storm, as the waves lapped gently against the shore, Isla knew her mission had only just begun. She would be the one to carry the message of the sea, to remind the world of the power that lay beyond human control. And perhaps, in time, the earth and sea would find balance once again.

Taniwha's Curse

The town of Vanaura had always been a peaceful place, nestled on the edge of a vast forest and overlooking a quiet bay where the ocean was a steady, calming presence. For generations, the people of Vanaura had lived in harmony with the land and sea, never venturing too far into either world, respecting the balance that had always existed. But one evening, that balance was shattered.

It began with a storm, one that seemed to come out of nowhere. Dark clouds rolled in swiftly, covering the sun and plunging the town into an unnatural twilight. The wind howled, and the waves crashed violently against the shore. As the storm raged, a mysterious figure appeared on the beach, carrying an old, weathered chest. The chest was adorned with strange symbols, none of which anyone in the town recognized. In the chaos of the storm, no one saw the man's face, but they saw the relic he carried—a relic of ancient design, unlike anything they had ever seen. As he approached the water, the ocean surged higher, and the storm reached its peak.

The man opened the chest, revealing a dark, pulsating stone at its center, and without warning, he hurled it into the waves. The moment the stone hit the water, the storm ceased as quickly as it had begun, leaving behind a silence so deep it felt unnatural. But the peace was short-lived.

By morning, strange things began to happen in Vanaura. The sea, once a peaceful neighbor to the town, now seemed to seethe with fury. The ocean grew restless, its waves crashing against the shore violently. Strange creatures washed up on the beach—large, mutated fish with glowing eyes, their bodies twisting unnaturally. Then, the people began to fall ill. They were plagued with vivid dreams of a great, serpentine creature rising from the depths, eyes burning with fury. The crops began to wither, and the once-fertile land started to dry up, as if the very life was being drained from the earth.

A curse had been unleashed.

The town, once thriving and full of hope, descended into chaos. The villagers whispered of the ancient myths, of the Taniwha, a guardian of the sea who had been forgotten by time. It was said that the Taniwha's power could be both a blessing and a curse. The relic, the stone that had been thrown into the sea, was known to be a part of an ancient ritual that bound the creature's power to the waters. To disturb it was to invite its wrath.

A group of five, each with their own reasons for risking everything, gathered in the town's hall. They had come together to find a way to undo the curse that had been unleashed upon them.

There was Kael, the scholar, whose knowledge of ancient myths had led him to recognize the symbols on the chest. He understood the legends surrounding the Taniwha better than anyone. Then there was Asha, a local healer, who had seen firsthand the toll the curse had taken on the people. She had lost loved ones to the strange afflictions that swept through the town. Beside her stood Bran, a fisherman, whose family had lived in Vanaura for generations. His connection to the sea was personal—his father had been one of the last to speak of the Taniwha before it was forgotten. The fourth member was Ilya, a warrior who had traveled far from another kingdom. She had heard whispers of the curse and knew that her skills would be needed to protect the group on their journey. Lastly, there was Marek, a former sailor who had witnessed firsthand the Taniwha's power when he was younger. He knew the sea's dark side and had the scars to prove it.

Together, they made their way to the beach, where the relic had been thrown into the water. Kael led the group, using his knowledge of the ancient rituals to guide them. The sea was still unsettled, its waves crashing unnaturally close to the shore, as if warning them to turn back.

"The relic must be returned to the sea," Kael said, his voice grim. "Only by returning it to the depths from which it came can we hope to lift the curse."

The group ventured into the water, the cold sea rising up to their waists as they waded deeper. As they moved toward the spot where the relic had been thrown, the sea seemed to react—dark shadows shifted beneath the water, and the ground trembled beneath their feet. They knew that the Taniwha was watching, aware of their presence.

Ilya drew her sword, her eyes scanning the water, her muscles tense, ready for anything. Asha spoke softly under her breath, offering prayers to the spirits of the sea, while Bran looked toward the horizon, his face set with determination.

Suddenly, the water surged, and from the depths, the Taniwha rose. It was massive, its serpentine form coiling through the water, its eyes glowing with an otherworldly light. The creature let out a deafening roar, sending a wave crashing toward them. Marek stumbled, nearly losing his footing, but he held onto the relic they had brought with them—a piece of ancient metal that had once been part of the chest. This was the key to returning the curse to the sea.

Kael stepped forward, his voice commanding. "Taniwha! We seek to return what was stolen. We seek to restore the balance."

The Taniwha's eyes locked onto him, and for a moment, the creature seemed to pause. Then, in a voice like the crashing waves, it spoke.

You seek to undo what has been done. But the curse cannot be undone so easily. The balance has been broken. The stone is no mere object—it is a part of me. A part of the sea. You cannot return it without consequence.

Kael's heart sank as the realization hit him. The stone was not just a relic—it was the Taniwha's heart, its essence. To return it would mean more than restoring balance—it would mean giving up the creature's power, the very force that had protected the oceans for centuries.

"You cannot ask for a return of the stone without understanding the cost," the Taniwha's voice rumbled. *What would you sacrifice?*

In that moment, it became clear to Kael what they had to do. The stone was tied to the Taniwha, yes, but it was also tied to the curse it had unleashed upon the world. To end the suffering, they would have to give up what they had come to seek: the Taniwha's power, and perhaps, their own chance at survival.

With a heavy heart, Kael lifted the relic high, casting it back into the deep. As it sank beneath the waves, the storm calmed, the water's fury subsiding. But as the waves retreated, so too did the Taniwha, disappearing into the ocean's depths, its power now lost forever.

The curse was lifted, but at a great cost. The ocean had taken what it was owed. And as the group returned to the shore, they understood that some powers, no matter how much they are revered or feared, must be allowed to fade in order to restore the balance.

The town of Vanaura would rebuild, but the lesson was clear: to disturb the natural order was to invite chaos. And in the end, the sea would always have the final say.

The Taniwha's Challenge

Darian had always known that he was meant for greatness. The youngest son of the village chieftain, he had spent his life watching his father lead, learning the ways of leadership, strategy, and diplomacy. His father, Aric, was respected by all, a wise man with the strength to command armies and the heart to unite disparate tribes. Darian, in contrast, was brash, eager, and driven by ambition. He knew that one day he would take his father's place, but as the years passed, the villagers started to doubt his readiness. They whispered that while he had the fire of youth, he lacked the wisdom that came with age.

It was the Taniwha who would decide whether Darian was ready.

For centuries, the Taniwha had been a figure of legend in their village, a creature of immense power who lived deep within the sacred lake at the foot of the mountains. It was said that the Taniwha could control the flow of rivers, summon storms, and could even glimpse into the future. The creature had always been revered, and its counsel was sought only in the most dire of circumstances. But the Taniwha had never interfered in the matters of the village until now.

One summer evening, as the sky darkened with the weight of an impending storm, the Taniwha emerged from the lake. Its eyes, glowing like molten gold, scanned the village with an intelligence that chilled Darian to his core. The villagers gathered at the water's edge, their hearts heavy with reverence and fear. And there, standing before the great beast, the Taniwha spoke.

"I have watched this village for centuries, and I have seen many leaders rise and fall," the creature's voice rumbled, its words echoing in Darian's chest. "But none have yet shown that they possess what it takes to lead this land into the future. I will not speak of your father, for he has already proven his worth. I will speak only of you, Darian. You seek to rule, but do you truly understand what it means to lead?"

Darian swallowed, stepping forward, his chest puffed out with the confidence that had always served him in the past. "I understand, Taniwha. I have studied my father's ways. I have listened to his counsel. I know what it takes to command the people and protect the land."

The Taniwha's eyes narrowed, and for a long moment, it studied Darian in silence, as if weighing his very soul. Then, with a deep, almost sorrowful sigh, the creature spoke again.

"Words are empty without action. The time has come for you to prove your worthiness. I will test you, young leader, in a challenge of wits and bravery. Succeed, and you shall prove yourself worthy of the title you seek. Fail, and you will know the consequences of your arrogance."

Darian's heart skipped a beat, but he was determined to rise to the occasion. "I accept your challenge, Taniwha. Whatever it may be, I will prove that I am worthy."

The Taniwha's gaze softened for a moment, as if pleased by Darian's bravado, before it spoke again. "You will venture into the heart of the mountain, where the Trial of the Four Winds awaits. There, you will face not only the forces of nature but the very doubts that plague your mind. If you return, victorious, with the wisdom of the winds, then you shall prove yourself worthy to lead."

The villagers murmured among themselves, unsure of the task before Darian. But the young man stood tall, his resolve unwavering. He had never backed down from a challenge, and this was no different. With a final nod to the Taniwha, he turned and began his journey toward the mountain.

The climb was grueling. The path was treacherous, and the winds howled with a power that made the trees bend and groan. But Darian pressed on, determined to face whatever trials awaited him. As he ascended higher into the mountain's peak, the winds grew fiercer, and soon, he found himself standing at the entrance of a cave, the Trial of the Four Winds waiting for him inside.

The first trial was the Wind of Intellect. The cave was vast, filled with ancient symbols and riddles carved into the walls. The wind howled within the cave, carrying with it the whispers of those who had come before. Darian knew that this was a test of his mind. He had always prided himself on his intelligence, but as he studied the riddles, his confidence faltered. The questions were complex, the answers hidden in the twisting, cryptic clues.

Hours passed, and Darian's frustration grew. He had never been one to sit idle, to ponder for too long. He was a man of action. But here, in the face of the riddle-filled cave, he realized that he couldn't force his way through. The Wind of Intellect demanded patience and focus. With a deep breath, he settled down and allowed his mind to quiet. Slowly, the answers began to reveal themselves, and with each solved riddle, he felt his mind expand, his understanding deepen. Finally, after what felt like an eternity, the Wind of Intellect receded, and Darian knew he had passed the first test.

The second trial was the Wind of Courage. The cave narrowed, and the air became thick and heavy. Dark shapes moved in the shadows, and the wind screamed as if to warn him. In the darkness, Darian could hear the sounds of footsteps—footsteps not his own. Shadows danced around him, shifting and changing, threatening to overwhelm him. The Wind of Courage wasn't just about fighting the darkness—it was about facing his own fears.

He closed his eyes and remembered his father's words: "True courage is not the absence of fear. It is the ability to stand in the face of fear and press forward."

With that thought, Darian stepped forward, his body trembling but his resolve firm. The shadows parted, and the wind eased. He had faced his fear and emerged stronger for it.

The third trial was the Wind of Compassion. In a small alcove within the cave, Darian found a dying creature—one of the very mutated fish that had plagued his village. The wind whispered to him, urging him to make a choice. He could end the creature's suffering with a quick blow, but in his heart, he knew that mercy was the key. He knelt beside the creature, offering comfort and soothing words, and in return, the creature's eyes gleamed with understanding before it peacefully passed away. The Wind of Compassion softened, and Darian knew he had passed.

Finally, the fourth trial was the Wind of Wisdom. The cave grew silent, the winds stilling as Darian approached the final chamber. In front of him was a pool of water, its surface perfectly still. But in its depths, he saw something far more than just his reflection. He saw his future—his failures, his doubts, his fears of inadequacy as a leader. The Wind of Wisdom did not ask him to defeat these thoughts; it asked him to acknowledge them.

Darian knelt by the water's edge and stared into the pool. With a deep breath, he allowed himself to accept the uncertainty of his path. Leadership was not about knowing all the answers, but about the willingness to grow and learn. And in that moment, the Wind of Wisdom embraced him, its power flowing through him.

When Darian returned to the Taniwha, it watched him silently for a long moment. Then, with a voice that resonated in his soul, the Taniwha spoke.

"You have faced the trials not with the arrogance of youth, but with the humility of wisdom. You have proven yourself worthy, not by defeating the challenges before you, but by embracing them."

Darian stood tall, understanding at last that true leadership came not from strength or force, but from wisdom, compassion, and the courage to face oneself.

The Taniwha's challenge had not just tested him—it had shaped him into the leader he was always meant to be. And as the creature disappeared into the sea, Darian knew that his journey had only just begun.

The Taniwha's Bridge

The village of Kaelora was perched at the edge of the land, where lush green hills met the dark expanse of the sea. The people of Kaelora had always lived with a sense of isolation. Though they revered the ocean, it was also a mystery—a vast, untamed force that they dared not fully understand. For centuries, the villagers had heard stories of the Taniwha, the great sea guardian, a creature whose power was said to be both a blessing and a curse. The Taniwha's name was spoken only in whispers, and its true nature was a subject of much debate. Some believed it to be a protector, others saw it as a threat.

One summer, a stranger came to Kaelora. He was a young man, lean and weathered by the sea, with eyes that glinted with curiosity and something darker, something deeper. His name was Eamon, and he had come seeking something that even the villagers didn't fully understand—a way to cross to the other side of the ocean.

"You've heard the tales, haven't you?" Eamon said, speaking to the village elders in the evening as they sat around the fire. "The Taniwha has built a bridge. A magical bridge that connects the land to the sea. And I've come to find it."

The elders exchanged nervous glances, their faces betraying their unease. "The Taniwha?" one of them muttered. "That's not something to chase after."

But Eamon was insistent. He had no family, no real home. The land beyond the sea held promises—of fortune, of answers, of something that called to him in ways he didn't quite understand. The villagers, though wary, could not stop him from pursuing his goal.

He spent the next several days wandering the cliffs, following the coastline, hoping to catch sight of the bridge. There was a strange energy in the air, an unspoken pull that seemed to guide him. It was as if the land itself was leading him toward something. On the seventh day, as the sun began to dip beneath the horizon, casting the sea in hues of orange and purple, he saw it.

Rising from the depths of the water, a shimmering arch stretched across the gap between land and sea. It was no ordinary bridge; its structure seemed to pulse with magic, as if it were alive. The stones that formed the bridge were slick and black, glistening like obsidian, and they sparkled with an ethereal light. The water around it was calm, the waves barely moving, as if the ocean itself had paused to honor the creation.

Eamon approached, his heart pounding with anticipation. As he set foot on the first stone, he felt a sudden shift in the air, a heavy weight settling on his chest. The bridge was not just a passage—it was a test. The Taniwha's magic was both a gift and a challenge, and Eamon could feel it.

"Who seeks to cross?" a voice rumbled from the depths, a voice that reverberated through his bones, like thunder that shook the earth itself.

Eamon froze, his breath catching. The Taniwha had spoken, but not in words. The voice was more like a presence, a force that filled the space around him. He felt it in his mind, in his heart—a pressure that demanded an answer.

"I seek to cross to the other side," he said, his voice firm despite the fear rising in his chest. "I have no intention to harm or steal. I wish only to pass."

There was a long silence, and Eamon felt as if the world was holding its breath, waiting for something—waiting for him to prove himself.

"You seek," the voice spoke again, but this time, it was softer, almost amused. "But you seek without understanding. The bridge is not for the greedy, nor for those who seek power. Only those with pure intentions may cross. Tell me, what do you truly desire?"

Eamon hesitated. He had no real answer. His desire for adventure, for answers, had always been tangled with ambition. His dreams of riches, of finding something that would make him more than just a wandering soul—hadn't he always wanted that? To be someone of importance, to escape his past?

He closed his eyes, taking a deep breath. "I seek... a place where I can belong," he said quietly, realizing that the words came from a deeper part of him. "A place where I am not just a shadow, where I can create something, make my mark."

The bridge seemed to shimmer in response, its light pulsing brighter for a moment before fading. The voice returned, this time gentle, yet firm.

"Your intentions are not pure, but they are honest," the Taniwha's voice said. "And honesty can be the foundation of true change."

Eamon's heart sank. He thought the Taniwha would deny him passage, but instead, the creature seemed to be reflecting something in him—something he had never truly understood about himself until that moment.

The ground beneath him shifted, and the bridge began to take on a new form. The stones began to shift, becoming more solid, more grounded. The path before him seemed to open up, yet it was unclear whether it was an invitation or a challenge. The Taniwha was offering him a chance to cross, but not without consequence.

"Proceed," the Taniwha said. "But remember: the journey you seek will not be what you expect. The other side is not what you imagine. It is a place where truth will be laid bare. And sometimes, to find a place to belong, one must first learn how to belong to themselves."

Eamon hesitated, feeling the weight of those words. He had sought the Taniwha's bridge to escape—to escape from the confines of his past, to find a better life on the other side. But the Taniwha had shown him something different. The truth was not in running away; it was in facing what lay within.

With a final glance back at the village—at the life he had come from—Eamon took his first step onto the bridge. This time, he did not feel the urge to flee. Instead, there was a calmness in him, a resolve he had never known before.

The Taniwha's challenge had been clear: to truly cross, he had to face himself. The bridge, a magical path between two worlds, was not simply a means to an end—it was a mirror, reflecting the truth of the traveler's heart.

As Eamon moved forward, the bridge shifted underfoot, and for the first time, he understood. The place he sought to belong to was not somewhere on the other side of the sea—it was within himself. And with that realization, he stepped into the unknown, his journey truly beginning.

The Taniwha watched from the depths, its eyes gleaming with approval.

Get Another Book Free

We love writing and have produced many books.

As a thank you for being one of our amazing readers, we'd like to offer you a free book.

To claim this limited-time offer, visit the site below and enter your name and email address.

You'll receive one of our great books directly to your email, completely free!

https://free.copypeople.com

Also by Morgan B. Blake

The Hidden Truth
Silent Obsession

Standalone
Temporal Havoc
The AI Resurrection
99942 Apophis
The Shadows We Keep
Whispers of the Forgotten
Christmas Chronicles: Enchanted Stories for the Holiday Season
Realm of Enchantment Tales from the Mystic Lands
The Taniwha's Secret